WHAT A WOMAN MUST DO

· Also by Faith Sullivan ·

Repent, Lanny Merkel

Watchdog

Mrs. Demming and the Mythical Beast

The Cape Ann

The Empress of One

Gardenias

Good Night, Mr. Wodehouse

WHAT A WOMAN MUST DO

a novel

Faith Sullivan

The characters and events in this book are fictitious. Any similarity to real persons, living or dead, is coincidental and not intended by the author.

First published by Random House, Inc., 2000.

Second paperback edition, published 2016 by Milkweed Editions
Printed in Canada
Cover design by Mary Austin Speaker
Cover painting by Edward Hopper, *Jo Painting* (1936)
Author photo by Sandra Kjarstad Bloom
16 17 18 19 20   5 4 3 2 1

978-1-57131-113-9

Milkweed Editions, an independent nonprofit publisher, gratefully acknowledges sustaining support from the Jerome Foundation; the Lindquist & Vennum Foundation; the McKnight Foundation; the National Endowment for the Arts; the Target Foundation; and other generous contributions from foundations, corporations, and individuals. Also, this activity is made possible by the voters of Minnesota through a Minnesota State Arts Board Operating Support grant, thanks to a legislative appropriation from the arts and cultural heritage fund, and a grant from the Wells Fargo Foundation Minnesota. For a full listing of Milkweed Editions supporters, please visit www.milkweed.org.

The following CIP data is from a previous edition.

Library of Congress Cataloging-in-Publication Data

Sullivan, Faith.
What a woman must do : a novel / Faith Sullivan.
p. cm.
ISBN 1-57131-037-1 (paper)
1. Women--Minnesota--Fiction. 2. Minnesota--Fiction. I. Title.
PS3569.U3469 W48 2002
813'.54--dc21

2002022668

Milkweed Editions is committed to ecological stewardship. We strive to align our book production practices with this principle, and to reduce the impact of our operations in the environment. We are a member of the Green Press Initiative, a nonprofit coalition of publishers, manufacturers, and authors working to protect the world's endangered forests and conserve natural resources. *What a Woman Must Do* was printed on acid-free 100% postconsumer-waste paper by Friesens Corporation.

For Irene, Marketa, and the Manion Family

Absence becomes the greatest Presence.

May Sarton

WHAT A WOMAN MUST DO

Harvester Standard Ledger

Wednesday, August 20, 1952

WAY BACK WHEN

Ten Years Ago. Archer and Celia Canby of this city died as a result of injuries sustained in a fiery crash at approximately 1:15 a.m., Sunday, when the car which Mr. Canby was driving left County Road 14, three miles north of Harvester. Mr. and Mrs. Canby are survived by their daughter, Elizabeth Katherine, age seven, and by Mrs. Canby's aunt, Katherine Drew, a long-time resident of this area.

CHAPTER 1

Katherine Drew

THE OLD ELMS, PLANTED DOUBLE and triple so that the trunks were as broad as the front end of a car, cast flickering patterns that promised, but did not deliver, relief from the August heat. Drooping limbs bowed indolently, ushering into the screen porch a shadow or possibly a shade.

Her cane hooked over the head of the daybed, Kate Drew lay like a sheaf of gnarled, dry twigs gathered into a blue chambray housedress. Her arms and legs were tinder ready to burst into flame, her joints throbbing coals. Turning over in bed raised sweat on her brow and brought stifled cries to her throat.

At the foot of the bed, where she'd flung it down, was the *Standard Ledger*. The piece about her niece Celia and Celia's damnable husband, Archer, had left Kate weak, and she'd lain down to catch her breath.

But what about Bess—the "daughter, Elizabeth Katherine" and Kate's grandniece? Before Bess came home from work, Kate would have to hide the paper.

Still, she supposed that the girl would have read it somewhere. Or someone would have told her about it. And Bess would know that Kate had read it. Kate always read the paper. All of it.

Well, a person had to, out of self-protection. In Harvester everybody knew everything about everybody, whether it was their business or not. In that way, it was different from the Cities or Chicago. Too different for Bess, Kate thought. Though her grandniece flounced around town pretending not to care what people thought (cursing and criticizing and smoking cigarettes), she was as sensitive as a tuberous begonia. She had to shock, and she had to be loved, and she didn't see that it was impossible to have it both ways.

When she was Bess's age, Kate had never needed to shock. But then she hadn't had anyone she needed to punish the way that Bess did. As for love, Kate hadn't given it much thought. It simply was, like water from a spring, pouring out of a cleft someplace in the universe. You held out your cup. You didn't worry about it.

My God, had she been that young, that ignorant?

At Bess's age (younger, actually), Kate had graduated at the head of her high school class, armed with a plan for getting back to the country. Her father had lost his farm to the bank after years of hard times and, despite ten-year-old Kate's wild tears and threats to throw herself from the hayloft, he had moved the family to town, where he'd worked as a carpenter for the rest of his life.

After graduation Kate caught a train to St. Cloud and teachers college. In return for room and board with her father's married niece, Elsie, she helped with the cooking and housework and looked after Elsie's three children. Despite all this, she managed to do well in her courses and have a good time. Elsie was young and dark and quiet, but full of little jokes and mysteries, and the two women got on well.

It was Elsie who had taught Kate to read the tea leaves and the cards. She called it "forecasting." "Forecasting" sounded practical, not like something that only gypsies did. Women friends came to have Elsie lay the cards out in mysterious arrangements on the kitchen table or swirl tea leaves in the cup. They didn't tell their husbands, nor did Elsie tell hers.

The first time that Elsie read Kate's tea leaves, she'd bent over the cup, intent as a biologist hunched over a microscope, then held the cup away from her to gain perspective and catch the light from the kerosene lantern.

Studying Kate's face, she murmured, "Yes . . ." and turned the cup this way, then that. If such a thing could be said, Elsie was scientific about the leaves: seen from different angles, patterns of leaves looked different and meant different things.

When she was at last satisfied that she understood the messages in the cup, Elsie tipped it toward Kate, saying, "Here is a man, tall and . . . fair, and a barn and . . . here is a ring, do you see it?" She held out the cup, pointing to the ring. "That means a wedding." She threw Kate a conspirator's grin. "I forecast that you're going to marry a farmer." She moved the lantern so that Kate could better see. "And the man, see here, is holding . . . a child's hand . . . a little girl's hand."

"And what is all this over here?" Kate wanted to know.

Elsie rose, carrying the cup to the sink. "That's . . . clouds . . . bringing rain to the farm."

wrenches them from their bed. Death tunnels beneath the earth or crawls along it or flies from the sky to threaten the lives of cabbages and calendula. No, she does not expect the garden to be easy, nor the farm. Like all of life, it is made up of small, sweet victories, maddening miscalculations, and horrid losses.

She is both a terrible romantic and a reluctant but dogged realist. The garden is worth all her tears and worries and tenderness, even as the larger fields of corn and rye are worth Martin's.

As she lies on the warm, dusty straw and gazes at the cornflower sky, the pleasure of the farm oozes through her and she moans softly, running her hands over her breasts and belly. Heaven will be a farm, she thinks. And we will own it outright.

Sitting up on her elbows, Kate gazes out toward the field where Martin is harrowing with Sunshine and Moonshine, one white horse, one black. A rush of gratitude sweeps over her. This farm belongs to Martin's family, and she is his wife. She is back!

Her roots reach down below the water table, as deep as the midnight world from which Demeter, goddess of agriculture, rescued her daughter Persephone. (This according to Unheard Melodies, *a slim book of Greek mythology, and Martin's boyhood prize for eight years of perfect school attendance.)*

Kate doesn't know where love for the farm leaves off and love for Martin begins. It is all of a piece—Martin, the earth, the giant, restless cottonwoods, the ripe, waiting feeling she has, lying here between rows of tomatoes, their succulent perfume caught in her hair, in the folds of her apron, in the pores of her skin.

Thank you, Martin, thank you for your hard work and your love and your farm.

She doesn't mind sharing the house with his old parents—Martin was born when his mother was nearly fifty. The old folks are kind and patient and teach Kate things she needs to know. His mother has taught her about herbs—baths and teas and balms and such—knowing which plants are good for what. Plantain for coughs and hoarseness, dill for upset stomach.

Though farm life is harsh, in winter especially, even winter is sensuous in its pregnant hoping and planning, in its stewardship of possibility. The family incubates possibilities through dark months while they are huddled in the kitchen, besieged by an invading army of cold and snow that sweeps across the prairie at the command of a tireless wind.

Kate sighs. The pond and the pails wait; the thirsty garden waits. The pond is spring-fed, and a twisting creek, narrow enough for a girl to leap, squeezes its way out, wriggling across the cow pasture.

Bounding to her feet, Kate runs, snatching up the pails from where they lie and the hem of her long skirts as well. Reaching the creek, she leaps it, then wheels, and leaps again.

Kate was awakened by her own thin moan. Though the day was warm, she was cold, except her burning joints. Quarter inch by quarter inch, she turned onto her side, dry bones hot inside her skin.

Closing her eyes and staring into the well of pain, she raised the young Kate slowly till she was sitting, manipulated the girl's legs and arms and torso thus and thus and thus, then lifted her to her feet.

Now, standing beside the daybed, trembling from the exertion, Kate reached for the head rail to steady herself. Beaded perspiration trickled from her forehead into the hairs of her black brows, and from her upper lip into the crease of her mouth. Her lips were pressed into a grimace of pain. Then, as she extracted a soft linen handkerchief from the sleeve of her dress and mopped her hairline and brows, her mouth twisted slowly into a thin smile of triumph.

CHAPTER 2

Harriet McCaffery

My, THAT'S A SMART-LOOKING BLOUSE," Harriet remarked to Estelle, the new girl in the office.

"Thank you. I got it at Penney's in St. Bridget."

"The ruffle around the neck suits your face."

Harriet thought maybe that kind of ruffle at the neck would be a good idea for *her*, what with her too-long and too-scrawny neck. She might think about getting one for herself, in a different color, of course. It wouldn't be fair to little Estelle if Harriet went out and bought the very same blouse.

Harriet liked, toward the end of the day, to visit a bit with the girls who worked under her. She thought it promoted morale. And besides, she liked the girls; she considered them friends. Not that she let them take advantage. She expected plenty of hard work from them, but who wanted to work for a grouch?

"You going to the Dakota tonight?" Martha asked. Martha had been with the Water and Power Company five years longer than Harriet, and tended to mother her.

"Rose asked me to her place for supper. We'll probably take a look in at the dance. Who's playing, do you know?"

Harriet was trying to sound offhand about the Wednesday-night dance at the Dakota Ballroom. She didn't want everybody knowing how she felt about the dances or, more to the point, how she felt about DeVore Weiss, who came to the dances at the Dakota. If nothing ever came of her and DeVore, she didn't want the girls feeling sorry for her. She wasn't one to wear her heart on her sleeve.

"Did you see this piece in the *Standard Ledger*?" Sue Ann asked Harriet. "It's about your people—Mrs. Drew's niece and her husband, the ones who died in the car accident."

How could that be? Harriet wondered. Celia and Archer had been dead ten years.

Sue Ann carried the paper back to Harriet's desk and laid it in front of her, open to page three and the "Way Back When" column.

"Right here," Sue Ann said, placing a Dare to Be Red fingernail on the "Ten Years Ago" item.

Why would they do this? Why would they rake it up again? You could bet your sweet life that if Kate owned a big business in town and advertised in the *Standard Ledger*, they'd have thought twice about running this item. It really made Harriet steam.

"You want me to cut it out so you can keep it?" Sue Ann asked.

"Yes." Why did she want to keep it? She didn't need reminders. Still, this was about her family. She'd lived with Kate Drew for twenty years. Kate was her second cousin once removed. And her family meant a great deal to

Harriet, so she would keep the clipping, even if she never looked at it again.

In 1932, Harriet, then nineteen and fresh from business college, had dropped in to visit Kate and Martin Drew, whom she saw every two or three years at family gatherings. From Sioux City, Iowa, she'd come, with a single pasteboard grip in her hand, and she'd stayed. Celia was eighteen then and still at home, though she was soon to marry Archer Canby.

Celia and Archer's accident had happened late on a Saturday night, Sunday morning, really, and the funeral was on Wednesday. Harriet, who was the bookkeeper at the Water and Power Company then, the job Sue Ann held now, hadn't come to work that week until Thursday. Harlan Bergson, the office manager in those days, hadn't been keen on Harriet's being out that long.

"It's not like it was your mother," he'd said.

Well, that just showed you how sensitive Harlan Bergson was. Kate had needed Harriet. Kate had just lost her husband the previous December—a heart attack the day Pearl Harbor was bombed. And now Celia was dead in a terrible accident—Celia, who was Kate's niece and her greatest joy. Of course Harriet had to be with Kate. And there was Bess to look after, Celia and Archer's seven-year-old daughter, a forlorn little thing who'd held on to Harriet's hand for the better part of three days. In Kate's condition, she couldn't look after Bess. Like a corpse herself, Kate lay in a darkened bedroom, under sedation.

What a fool that Harlan Bergson had been. Who did

he think was going to make funeral arrangements for Celia and Archer and pick out the coffins and the printed programs and thank-you's? Because of the condition of the bodies, there could be no viewing, of course, but there would be a wake. Who would see that it went smoothly and that Kate didn't tire herself too much? Who, if not Harriet?

She hoped that in *her* years as office manager, she'd never been as callous as Harlan Bergson. Well, she thought, it wasn't Christian of her to think bad of the man. He'd been drafted shortly after the funeral and killed later on the island of Okinawa. Harriet had been promoted to office manager because there weren't any men around, and she'd hung on to the job even after the war, thank God. And why not? She was the best-qualified person at the Water and Power Company. She had a diploma from business college and she was sharp, sharper even than Mr. Dorsey, the big boss. She was always having to fill him in on what was what.

Harriet took the "Way Back When" clipping from Sue Ann and slipped it into her purse. Maybe she should change her plans for supper and the dance. Maybe she should stay at home with Kate tonight. Though she hated coddling, Kate was bound to be upset by the item in the paper. When Harriet got home from work she would see how Kate was feeling.

When she thought of all the grief that Archer Canby had caused, Harriet had to shake her head.

The night of the accident, Harriet had answered the doorbell at about 2:00 A.M. to find Constable Wall standing on the porch, crying.

"Harriet," he said, "that son of a bitch has killed her."

Gus Wall and his wife, Marie, had lived on the corner diagonally across the street from the Drews all the years since Kate and Martin and Celia had moved to town. Harriet had opened the screen door and he'd come in, blowing his nose and clearing his throat. She knew right away who had killed whom. There wasn't a moment's doubt that Archer had killed Celia.

"How? Where?" she asked, pulling her robe around her and shivering although the night was hot and still. "Where's Archer?"

"He's dead, too. Car accident out at the Jessups'. They hit a tree. Archie Voss and I decided Kate shouldn't see 'em." Mr. Voss was the mortician. "Will you make the identification?"

After calling Cousin Frieda to come stay with Kate, Harriet went up to Kate's bedroom and wakened her. The first thing Kate said was "Something's happened to Celia." It was like everyone had always known that something would happen. Archer Canby was doom waiting to happen.

Back in 1932, when Celia had married Archer and moved out, Harriet had been with the Drews only a few months. Over the following years, she and Celia, who were nearly the same age, had grown fond of each other, but they had never become what Harriet would call close, and Celia had never confided in Harriet why she stayed with Archer.

Harriet wasn't one for divorce, but she thought most women would have left Archer Canby. Harriet had finally concluded that Archer had been a kind of obsession of

Celia's, a madness. Women did lose their sanity over men, and men over women. You couldn't call it love, could you?

Mr. Voss had a whiskey ready for Harriet in his office when she was done identifying the bodies. But she was sick as soon as she drank it, and she hadn't been able to put much more than weak tea in her stomach for a couple of days.

When Harriet returned to the house that morning, Dr. White had come and gone. Cousin Frieda had called him, and he'd given Kate something to calm her. But Kate hadn't gone right back to bed. She'd put on a robe and was sitting in the kitchen on the stool, ripping rose-colored trim from the neck and pockets of an old black percale dress.

Harriet and Frieda stayed with her awhile, but along toward 4:00 A.M., when the sky had begun to lighten, Kate said, "Don't hang around. Go to bed." She wanted to be alone.

For Harriet, the worst part of the night was watching Kate sit by the window ripping the trim from that old black dress. She'd rip a section, then stare out the window as if a car might yet pull into the drive from the alley. Then she'd rip another bit. She wore nothing but black for the next two years.

Could anyone tell Harriet why a newspaper would print such a story ten years later and bring it all back? It was criminal. She looked up the number for the *Standard Ledger* and picked up the receiver.

"Seven-three-eight, please," she told the operator.

"*Ledger*. Can I help you?"

"I want the person who does the 'Way Back When' column, please."

A young male voice came on the line. "Can I help you?"

"My name is Harriet McCaffery and I'm related to the Drew family. You carried a piece about them, about a car accident, in the 'Way Back When' section, and I want to know why you would do that. Both Katherine Drew and Bess . . . *Elizabeth* Canby still live in this town. Can you imagine how they're going to feel, reading that?"

"I just moved here a month ago, Mrs. McCaffery. I don't know the Drews or anybody else. I'm sorry if I chose a piece you don't like or a piece that'll upset somebody. But I'm just told to find interesting copy from the back numbers."

"Well, don't you ever check something before it gets in the paper?"

"Mr. Hardesty, the publisher, is up at Leech Lake on vacation with his family. We're doing the best we can down here. I'm sorry if I upset you. I don't know what else to say. I'd think that after ten years these people would be, well, past it by now."

"Let me tell you, young man, I identified the bodies. Mrs. Canby had been decapitated and Mr. Canby's face was gone. Do you think that's something people get past?"

Harriet hung up the phone on him. She didn't think she'd hung up on someone twice in her life, but really . . . the girls were looking at her. She began to tidy her desk. When they saw her put the cover on her typewriter, they started closing drawers, extinguishing desk lamps, and blowing eraser crumbs off the tops of their desks.

As Martha started out the door, she called back to Harriet, "If you see DeVore Weiss tonight, tell him hello from me and my mister."

Now, how had Martha known about DeVore Weiss? I must be as transparent as a window, Harriet thought.

CHAPTER 3

Elizabeth Canby

THE SUPPER CROWD AT THE LOON CAFE had been pretty thin, so Dora let Bess Canby go early. Dora didn't like her waitresses standing around looking for customers who probably weren't coming. And if she was going to let somebody go early, it was going to be Bess, not Shirley, Dora's niece. Pay the wages to family.

Bess didn't care. The Loon Cafe was hot and greasy. In the winter the grease went up to the tin ceiling. In August it settled on your skin like a coat of Vaseline.

Bess picked up the copy of the *Standard Ledger* lying on the counter where customers could read it when they came in for coffee. Dora always had two copies for the customers.

"It's okay if I take this?" Bess asked.

"Sure. Nothin' in it."

Dora never read the "Way Back When" column. What did she care what happened ten years ago or twenty or a hundred? "Fifty years ago Mr. and Mrs. Bill Smith of Red Berry were guests of Mr. and Mrs. Anson Obermeier of this city on Saturday evening. Mrs. Smith and Mrs. Obermeier are cousins," she'd read aloud one afternoon, laughing and tossing the paper on the counter. "Who cares what happened back then? Nobody gives a hoot." But plenty of people cared. They read the column. They remembered. They gave a hoot.

When Bess had read the "Ten Years Ago" item about Celia and Archer that afternoon, she'd been furious. Wasn't that the cruelest, stupidest goddamned thing you could think of, rehashing a story about people's deaths ten years ago? Great-aunt Kate had seen it by now, Bess was sure. The paper was delivered on Wednesday afternoon. Aunt Kate always read it as soon as it came. Every last column.

In a sense Bess hadn't been surprised by the piece. Cousin Frieda had said a week or so ago, "It's nearly ten years." But why stir up everyone else's memories? In a little place like Harvester, the past never became *history*, but sat side by side with current events, like an old woman pushing in among the young ones, insisting on being a part of things.

Bess thrust open the screen door of the Loon Cafe and stepped out into the blazing six-thirty shimmer of Main Street. The street was nearly deserted but she sauntered along with uneasy disdain as though, the item having been delivered to everyone's doorstep that afternoon, many eyes would be fixed upon her, waiting for her to stumble.

When Bess slammed the kitchen screen door at six-forty, her great-aunt was puzzled. "Thought you were working till eight," she said.

"Not enough customers."

"I didn't fix supper, just a slice of melon and an ear of corn. Too hot. I'll put something on for you. Only take a minute." Kate pushed herself up from the dining room table.

"I'm not hungry, just thirsty," Bess told her. "I'll get some iced tea."

Kate's copy of the *Standard Ledger* was conspicuously missing from the dining room, hidden in her desk or in the sideboard, and she had not remarked on Bess's copy lying on the table with her purse.

Kate followed Bess into the kitchen, carrying the plate with the denuded cob and green melon rind on it. "Harriet's having supper at Rose's. They're going to the dance."

"At the Dakota?" Bess asked.

"I expect."

"But it's Old Time tonight."

"She's been going to the Old Time dances all summer," Kate observed, sprinkling pepper along the melon rind. Rind didn't draw ants, she said, if you sprinkled pepper on it before you put it into the garbage.

Her cousin Harriet had always hated the Wednesday-night dance at the Dakota. It was oompah music, polkas and schottisches and country waltzes. "A bunch of perspiring, red-faced Germans mopping their brows and blowing big horns," Harriet sniffed. "Educated people don't go to Old Time. It's bad enough at the Dakota on the weekends when the music is modern, but Wednesday nights are . . . common." "Common" was Harriet's most damning epithet, one she'd picked up from Aunt Kate. "Common" was anything not to Harriet's tastes, and she was a woman of exceedingly refined tastes, having graduated from business college as well as high school.

Purple, orange, and lime green were *common* colors. Women who had their ears pierced were *common*. Men who didn't snap the front of their hat brims down, but had them turned up all the way around, were *common*, and so were men who wore white socks to church.

Oompah music was common. Yet here was Harriet, off to the Wednesday-night Old Time dance at the Dakota Ballroom, trailing Tabu through a sea of Evening in Paris. Unless she had to sit near the restrooms. Near the restrooms even Tabu could not fight its way through the reek of urine.

Bess stood by the refrigerator drawing the cold tea glass across her forehead and hating the greasy smell of her tan Loon Cafe uniform. Aunt Kate sat on a high stool across the kitchen, plucking withered leaves from African violets on the windowsill.

"She started going to Old Time night about six months after DeVore Weiss's wife passed away," Kate said.

"DeVore Weiss? The one who farms over by Ula?"

"The same."

"Jesus H. Christ." She leaned heavily against the refrigerator and stared at her glass, two fine lines appearing between her brows.

"Don't swear. It sounds common."

"DeVore Weiss is an old man."

"He's . . ." Kate stopped to calculate. "He's forty-some. He was two or three years ahead of your mother in high school, so he's not much older than Harriet."

"And he's got kids still living at home," Bess went on, unimpressed by the arithmetic. DeVore's son Lyle was a year behind Bess in school, and another son, Delwin, was a year behind him. Tall, rawboned boys with crimson cheeks and hands and ears, they laughed at themselves and everyone else. Bess was sure they were simple, but they were passed to the next grade every year.

As if the glass were suddenly too heavy to hold, Bess set it on the Hoosier cupboard. "My God, can you see Harriet married to a farmer and with his kids at home? She'd have a nervous breakdown making sure nobody tracked manure in on their shoes. Why would she want that? She's got a job."

Kate smiled, then raised a dish towel to her face to cover the smile. "I never said she was getting married. But, if she did, what's wrong with that? She's not a spring chicken. She doesn't want people calling her an old maid. You know her well enough to know that."

"I wouldn't care if people called me an old maid, not if I had my own money." Bess thrust out a hip defiantly.

"It's my impression that Harriet's fond of DeVore."

"Anyway, calling somebody an old maid is dumb," Bess pressed sullenly. "I'd rather be an old maid and work at the Water and Power Company than be married to DeVore Weiss."

"Pride is cold in bed."

"Hot-water bottles are cheap. There's worse things than being a virgin."

"What do you know about worse things than being a virgin? What have *you* been up to?" her aunt asked without worry.

Kate knew that Bess was a virgin. She'd been concerned

last winter when Bess was seeing Jack Comstock, but after she'd broken off with him in April, Kate had asked her if she was crying because she'd gone too far with Jack, and Bess had said, "I'm crying because I didn't." They'd laughed at that.

Bess later reasoned that if she'd been able to maintain her virgin state with Jack Comstock, who was a prairie Adonis, then he was not *it.* When she met *it,* she wouldn't have a will of her own. On the other hand, if she never met *it,* she would have her maidenhead intact forever. And she would rather sleep in the coldest single bed in Minnesota for all eternity than go looking for something at the Old Time dances.

"I think it's disgusting," she said, "if Harriet's dancing polkas just so she can see DeVore Weiss. It's . . . it's shabby and dishonest. And . . . and *pathetic.*"

Snatching the iced-tea glass from the cupboard, she fled the kitchen, grabbing the *Standard Ledger* and her purse from the dining room table. She mounted the stairs, hands shaking, tea slopping on the wooden steps as she went. "Disgusting."

And indeed Bess was sickened. She'd never thought of Harriet leaving. Harriet McCaffery, with her scrawny neck and her pretensions, was part of an indivisible family: Bess, Aunt Kate, and Harriet.

When Bess left Harvester to go to college, and later, when she started an exciting job God only knew where—maybe London—and married some highly educated man who smoked a pipe and had leather patches on the sleeves of his tweed jackets, it was Aunt Kate and Harriet who would weep, wish her well, and welcome her back for visits; Aunt Kate and Harriet who would write long letters about Harvester and the cousins and neighbors; Aunt Kate and Harriet to whom Bess would write tissuey airmail letters about punting on the . . . Cam? . . . and about her "flat" and Albert Hall and the Lake Country.

Out there, in the world, was *life*—possibilities rushing toward you, too bold and lush to be imagined without the breath catching in your throat. Back here, in Harvester, was only the known and knowable: that which could be readily grasped and, like bread dough, easily punched down to its small, familiar stickiness.

Bess would write to Aunt Kate and Harriet about the world out there, sharing its fabulous monuments and subtle charms. Kate and Harriet's world would expand as Bess shared hers.

How could Harriet, then, run after DeVore Weiss as though she didn't care a damn about being in this family? As though she had no responsibilities here?

Bess sat down at the dressing table made of orange crates and dotted swiss, like one in *Seventeen* magazine, and looked at herself in the mirror. To whom did she belong if not to Aunt Kate and Harriet? And didn't they belong to her?

Most of the time Bess felt strong and grown up, even sophisticated, by Harvester standards. But when someone left you, she thought, part of you sickened and shrank. Oh, you revived enough to go to work or school, but you

and Donna Olson, along with several other girls in her class, the Class of '52. Two of them, Betty Beswick and Melva Hardy, were already married. Sad, wasn't it?

But not so sad as the thought of Harriet marrying DeVore Weiss. How sad and disgusting that was. How common.

CHAPTER 4

Kate

REACHING FOR HER CANE, Kate made her way to the screen door, pushing it open and standing for a minute on the back step, looking at the grass, which needed mowing, and the garden, which wanted weeding. Her arthritis made both tasks impossible. Harriet helped sometimes on Sunday afternoons, but she always made such a project out of it, tying on a big, floppy straw hat like one she'd seen Greer Garson wearing in a movie, and donning gloves! Only in movies did women wear gloves to pull crabgrass.

And Kate didn't like to ask too much of Harriet. After all, she paid room and board. Fleetingly Kate considered that that would stop if Harriet got married. She would have to find another boarder. But if DeVore Weiss was what Harriet wanted, Kate hoped she got him, though shepherding another woman's children through the teenage years didn't seem like the most romantic way to spend a honeymoon. And Harriet was an awful romantic, a deprived romantic.

Maybe Bess would mow the lawn Sunday morning. She didn't attend the Methodist Church anymore, hadn't since they'd buried Celia and Archer. The church seemed connected in Bess's mind with all the rebuffs and losses she had suffered.

Well, Kate couldn't deny that the accident had been a scandal among the Methodists, among the other denominations as well. The culminating scandal. And Bess was too young to understand that *every* family had its scandals sooner or later. The sure knowledge that this was true made living in a small town tolerable.

Archer had been drunk. Folks who'd been at the ballroom that night soon broadcast their firsthand accounts around church and around St. Bridget County. Archer had been drunk many times, and he was mean when he was drunk. Kate had thought it was because of his withered arm and being a southerner among closemouthed northerners. But there was something more, something born in his bones: a simple and awful predilection to grievance, not merely a willingness but a desire to find injury.

Whether driven by injury or not, destroying himself so wantonly and taking his young wife along was a thing that couldn't be forgiven. Even if she could have forgiven Archer for Celia, Kate couldn't forgive him for Bess. In a place like Harvester, scandal was a stain that time did not bleach.

Kate stepped down into the yard, leaning on her cane and holding on with her free hand to the sturdy trellis where purple clematis leaped from lath to lath. She couldn't go into the yard without her cane now. Only fifty-nine last February and already she was half crippled with arthritis.

Slowly, carefully, her back held as straight as a plumb line, she moved toward the bench by the lilacs. Getting down and back up again would be an awful chore, but she wanted to sit here and watch the last of the sun.

Yet, when she was settled, and her eyes swept the fiery opal sky in the west, thoughts of Archer clouded her sight. He was never far from her, but tonight he hovered, taunting. She gave her head a wry twist as though to shrug him away.

To go on hating him year after year wasn't Christian, of course. But she had made a deal with God about that. If she lived to see Bess safely off to college, without a dreadful mishap that could in any way be laid at Archer's headstone, she would forgive the man.

Giving up the burden of hate would be a relief. In fact, she believed that the arthritis had come from carrying that burden. God was telling her that hate was onerous and painful. Still, she would mind her own stubborn agenda, shouldering her ill will until Bess was safe.

Lifting a thin, twisted hand, blue knotted veins lacing its parts together, Kate touched the back of her head where it ached and stared unseeing at the gladiola bed.

Her eyes narrowed. Not long after Celia had married him, an ugly tale had surfaced regarding Archer Canby. If only Kate had known of it before the wedding. She never told Celia and she didn't know if anyone else had. Kate had only got wind of it through Cousin Frieda. Even now she did not like to give it room in her thoughts. It was too sad.

Enough. Stamping the earth impatiently with the cane, the old woman set her jaw and arched her back, seeking some arrangement of her bones that would ease the pain.

she went there, or how much 3.2 it took to affect a girl's judgment.

Most of Bess's senior crowd went, Kate knew, and if she forbade it, Bess would go anyway. Kate didn't like it, though. It wasn't the beer. Two or three bottles of beer weren't going to ruin anyone. During Prohibition she herself had brewed homemade beer for the family, putting it up in old ketchup bottles. No, it wasn't that.

And it wasn't the senior boys. She didn't give them credit for any more morals or self-restraint than they possessed, but if Bess hadn't been persuaded by Jack Comstock, she wasn't going to be persuaded by any of them.

What elusive danger, then, waited in the Lucky Club? A chill like an electrical current passed through Kate, and she rubbed her arms with fingers like gnarled roots.

The item in the *Standard Ledger*, that was what had put her on edge. But Bess wasn't Celia.

Bess crossed the yard and kissed Kate's cheek. Kate grasped the girl's firm arm. "If you and Donna go in a car with boys, don't let them drive fast."

"Oh God, Aunt Kate, I'm not going to get in an accident."

"And don't swear," Kate teased, trying to send the child off with a smile. "Men will think you're loose."

CHAPTER 5

Bess

BESS SET OUT NORTH along Second Street, waving to Cousin Frieda, whose house lay across the street from Kate Drew's and next door to Constable Wall's on the corner. Cousin Frieda, nearly as old as Kate, kept everything so clean, her place was an Exhibition of Cleanliness. The grass, dark and unpocked by dandelions, was short and springy, dazzlingly unsoiled. The sidewalk appeared scrubbed, and indeed Frieda did scrub it sometimes, on her hands and knees with a big brown brush. The front windows, westward facing, sparkled in the dying sunset and gave back reflections as unclouded as Frieda's conscience.

Frieda, in a starched cotton housedress and starched apron, sat in a rocker on the front porch. She lifted a strong, red hand, waving to Bess across Second Street.

"Bess," she called.

"Cousin Frieda."

"Your grandma alone tonight?"

"Yes." Bess paused in front of the McNaughton house. "Guess I'll call her to come play bridge. Harriet home?"

"No."

"I'll call Marie then."

Marie was Constable Wall's wife. The fourth would be Arnold, Frieda's husband and the proprietor of Drew's Body and Lube, once owned by Kate's husband, Martin, and his cousin Arnold together.

"See you, Cousin Frieda."

The woman rose and hurried into the dim recesses of her lemon-smelling house to phone Kate and Marie, and also to tell Arnold to drive downtown and pick up chocolate ice cream at Anderson's. All this Bess knew, because it was as it had always been, and as it was supposed to be. She glanced at the Bulova Harriet had given her for graduation—seven forty-five—and turned left toward the school and Donna.

She and Donna had been babies together, their mothers good friends. Before her parents' accident, Bess had lived in the little five-room bungalow next to Donna's house. Afterward, Mr. Albers, who owned the bungalow, had sold it to James Timm, the new manager of the grain elevator. Timm and his wife were quiet, childless Holy Rollers who needed nothing bigger than the five small rooms. Even that had seemed excessive. They took up very little space. The house did not embrace them as it had Celia and Bess.

Bess had not been inside the place since it was sold. She loved it, more than when it was her own, but refused every opportunity to step inside. The most recent occasion had come one dark, frigid afternoon late last January.

She and Donna were trudging house to house selling cookies to raise money for the senior trip, and Mrs. Timm had invited them in out of the numbing weather while she fetched her purse. Donna opened her mouth to accept the offered warmth, but Bess lied abruptly, "We're not supposed to enter customers' homes."

How could she stand to see her darling bungalow in the tepid embrace of the Timms? However mild and blameless they were, Bess would always hate them for living in her house. The first thing she would do when she was rich was buy the place back.

Did the house understand that she'd been forced to leave and that she would return for it? Did the dainty rooms recall the touch and sound of her and Celia and Archer?

As she grew older and her parents did not, Bess thought of them as Celia and Archer, not Mommy and Daddy. In a few years she would be older than they, and they would become her children.

The evening was hot and still. Front-room lights were not turned on, and kitchen lights were extinguished as soon as dishes were washed. People sat on porches or in backyards. They laughed or argued softly, or maybe the heavy air muffled the sounds. Even the squeals of children at the corner playing kick the can floated watery and muted.

The night that Celia and Archer died, it had been hot. Bess remembered that. She remembered it all. They had left her at Aunt Kate's while they went to the dance at the Dakota.

Bess had been very tired, so tired that she cried without reason after Celia left her at the door. When she had undressed down to her underwear, Kate rocked her in the little rocker in Kate's bedroom and recited nursery rhymes.

Bess's favorite was about a Queen of Hearts who made some tarts that were stolen by a knave. And the King of Hearts beat the knave and got the tarts back. But each time that Kate recited the rhyme, she ended by hugging Bess and laughing, "Of course, it was really the Queen who beat the knave and got the tarts back. No woman who bakes tarts and has them stolen would wait around for her husband to fetch them! Oh my, no."

Bess had fallen asleep on her aunt's lap and Kate had carried her to bed in the room that was now hers.

Because of the heat, Bess had slept without a gown or a sheet, but a cool, sweet breeze had come up about four-thirty, rustling the branches of the elms outside the bedroom windows and waking her with a chill.

"Mommy's soul woke me," she later told Donna, explaining the breeze. "On the way to heaven, she woke me up."

The grackles were already arguing next door in the McGiverns' backyard when Bess pulled on the cotton nightie she kept at Kate's and crept downstairs to sit on the front steps and watch the sun come up. Sunrise was a magician's trick, the drama of which did not diminish with repetition.

In the kitchen, where she'd intended to pour herself a bowl of puffed wheat, Bess found Aunt Kate in a horrid old black percale dress that she almost never wore. The pocket was mysteriously gone, along with the rose-colored trim. Tiny frizzed bits of thread clung to the dress where the trim had been torn away. Kate sat staring out the window at the alley as if waiting for a car to pull into the drive.

"Your mama and daddy died in an accident last night," Kate said without turning toward Bess. "The car went off the road and hit a tree."

Bess continued out the back door and sat on the step. She could not think or feel. When at length an intact thought surfaced, it was *The car went off the road. Cars don't decide to go off the road. Somebody drives them off.*

They had gone away and left her, as if she were something negligible that could be abandoned, like an old doll. What now? What about her house? Could she go on living there, renting it from Mr. Albers? Would they let her do that? But where would she get the $20 a month for the rent?

In the months following the funeral, Donna Olson and Donna's parents had stuck by Bess. They had invited her to dinner and to stay the night at least once a week. Some days Aunt Kate had been unable to look at Bess or talk to her, and the Olsons had understood and had taken her to their house, next door to her own dear bungalow, which was dark and silent, shades drawn, like eyes closed against tears.

Now Donna was waiting on the granite steps of the school, her pink-and-white-striped sundress spread out around her. Donna was a generous, giggling girl with one quirk: she liked to pose as she saw movie stars posed in fan magazines and films. When you came upon her sitting or standing, you were struck by her physical attitude, and couldn't help wondering who she was this time. She posed as an exercise in self-improvement, presenting to the world a persona more arresting or alluring than she imagined herself to possess.

Tonight's portrait, Bess intuited, was Olivia De Havilland as Melanie in *Gone With the Wind.* Cousin Harriet had taken Bess and Donna to see the movie in Sioux Falls when it had come back last year on a return engagement. Melanie was Donna's favorite film character, and something about the way that Donna had spread her dress out, and tilted her head just so, conjured that tragic southern belle, whom Bess considered impossibly virtuous and sappy.

"God, that's a neat sundress," Bess observed. "Did you get it in St. Bridget?"

"My mom made it from a Simplicity pattern," Donna told her, brushing the back of the skirt. "You can borrow the pattern, if you want."

Behind the school and across Fifth Avenue lay the park with its band shell, where the summer concerts were played. The park was filling with folks fleeing the oppression of stuffy rooms, where the odor of last week's liver and onions met the ghost of cigars Grandpa had smoked before the Second World War.

"Let's sit over there," Donna suggested, pointing her bag of popcorn toward a row of spirea bushes near one of the park entrances. "There's Neddy Barnstable," she observed, nodding in the direction of a young man home from his sophomore year at Yale. "He's a god," she sighed.

Mr. Hanson, the band director, though two minutes early, flustered importantly across the forestage of the band shell to the podium as though he were late and expecting a restive audience to fold up its blankets and steal away. With a great intake of breath and a harried glance toward the languid gathering, he mopped his brow with a dish towel–size handkerchief, gave a slight and preoccupied bow, then tapped the baton ferociously against the music stand as the band tuned up.

At length "The Star-Spangled Banner" burst forth from the shell and the audience grunted to its feet, all except the three people in wheelchairs: the smartly dressed Mrs. Herbert Hanlon, whose paralysis Bess knew nothing about; Bess's distant cousin Caroline, who'd been stricken with polio in 1948; and Orville Nelson, linotype operator at the *Standard Ledger* and World War One veteran, who'd been in a wheelchair since 1918. Orville always wept when the national anthem was sung. When she was little, Bess had cried along with him.

When the song ended, everyone sat down on the grass to swat mosquitoes and hum along with Gershwin, Lehár, and Sousa. Babies crawled and complained on their blankets; little children ran and hid behind trees, then made pilgrimages to the popcorn stand, and fell asleep with their heads on their fathers' laps. At the fringe of the park a pair of lovers, Sue Ann Meyers, who worked with Harriet, and Arvin Winetsky, stood silhouetted against the waning twilight, their arms linked.

Neither Bess nor Donna had been a member of the high school band, though both had been majorettes. Bess, however, had played the piano for nine years, beginning when she was five. Celia's piano.

When Bess was six, Celia had heard her putting

melodies to Mother Goose rhymes. "Are those pieces that Mrs. Rayzeen assigned?" she asked, hearing the child plink out a sad little melody as she sang a familiar rhyme about poor babes in the woods.

Bess shook her head.

"Where did you learn them?"

"I make them up," Bess huffed as though she found the question insulting.

"Really? Do you like making up music?"

Bess nodded, resuming the song.

"That's a very nice song. Do you know how to write the notes on paper?"

"Yes." She was growing impatient. This conversation was interfering with her work.

"Will you write down the notes to this song?"

"Not till I get them the way I want them. Now, Mommy, you're interrupting."

Smiling, Celia turned away. "I'm sorry."

After Celia's death the piano had come back to Aunt Kate's house and, until three years ago, Bess had found solace in it.

Mrs. Stubbs had ruined that.

Bess had taken lessons first from Mrs. Rayzeen, whose husband owned the lumberyard, and later, after Mrs. Rayzeen's throat cancer was discovered, from Mrs. Stubbs, whose husband was killed on Omaha Beach.

It was soon after Celia and Archer's deaths, when Bess was seven, that she'd begun the lessons with Mrs. Stubbs. Like Mrs. Rayzeen before her, the new piano teacher had made a fuss over Bess's playing and exclaimed over her interest in composition, writing notes home to Kate about Bess's talent, regretting that Sioux Falls was so far away, as Bess ought to have composition lessons from a certain professor at Augustana College.

Smitten with the young Mrs. Stubbs, Bess brought the teacher little treats, fudge or cookies or Black Jack gum. She let her hair grow long like Mrs. Stubbs's, and each week presented her with a composition, usually with accompanying lyrics full of coincidence and irony. She devoured the teacher's praise and criticism, hurrying home after every lesson to rework what she'd written and begin a new effort.

Playing her own compositions as well as those assigned by Mrs. Stubbs, Bess was featured prominently at recitals by the time she was ten.

Then one day when she was in the ninth grade, Bess plunged into the house after school, slamming the back door and gasping for air. Dumping an armload of books onto the dining table and snatching a sheaf of compositions from the piano, she hurled herself up the stairs. In the bathroom, she hacked off her long hair, wrapping it in the compositions and setting fire to it in the pink metal wastebasket that Harriet had bought.

"What on earth is going on?" Aunt Kate demanded.

"I'm quitting piano lessons."

"What?"

"Nancy Proess overheard Mrs. Stubbs in Truska's Grocery Store talking to somebody—she doesn't know who—and saying Bess Canby's stuck on herself and not that good a piano player, either."

"And you believed Nancy Proess?"

"Why would she lie?"

"I don't know. Maybe she's jealous. There could be plenty of reasons. I for one don't believe that Mrs. Stubbs said that. Get on the phone and ask her."

"No."

"You're not going to ask her?"

"No."

When Bess failed to show up for her next lesson, Mrs. Stubbs called, inquiring if Bess were ill.

Kate explained what had happened.

Mrs. Stubbs insisted that she'd never said any such thing about Bess, and that she was going to have a word with Nancy. She would get to the bottom of this.

And she did have a word. Nancy denied that she'd said anything.

Several times Mrs. Stubbs phoned the house, asking to talk to Bess, but Bess wouldn't take the receiver, and eventually the teacher stopped calling.

Bess closed the hinged lid of Celia's piano and didn't open it again.

As the piano had done, band concerts brought Celia back to Bess. Every Wednesday summer evening, weather permitting, Celia had brought Bess to the park. And since Aunt Kate didn't suffer from arthritis in those days, she came along too, lounging on a faded red-and-blue Indian blanket.

When Great-uncle Martin was alive, before Pearl Harbor, he whiled away Wednesday nights playing snooker with the old men at the Huntsman Beer Tavern and Pool Hall, nursing a beer and smoking a cigar. He always arrived home by ten o'clock, bringing with him a bag of mints and a couple of packs of Black Jack gum from Anderson's Candy and Ice Cream.

On the way home from the concert, Bess and Celia stopped at Aunt Kate's to say hello to Uncle Martin. He gave the candy and gum to Bess, and Kate sent something home with Celia, half a cake or a package of chops or a jar of rhubarb-strawberry preserves.

Like Uncle Martin, Archer didn't attend the concerts. But he did not play snooker. Instead, he usually sat at home. The band was terrible, he said; he could hear better on WCCO or at the Dakota Ballroom. Sometimes he went to the ballroom while Bess and her mother were out, even though he wasn't fond of Old Time. Of the Wednesday-night bands he complained, "I don't know why they don't play cowboy music instead of them damned butterflies." The butterfly was a dance with two men and one woman, or two women and one man, and Bess thought it was beautiful. Still, Archer went to Old Time to aggravate them all. And afterward he picked a fight with Celia.

"Why can't you come to the dance with me?" he would ask.

"I can't ask Aunt Kate to take care of Bess two and three nights a week so I can go dancing. Besides, I don't like Old Time."

"You too *good* for Old Time? You'd rather do your high-tone lady act. Lemonade and sour music with a flock of old hens."

"I like the concerts. I like to be with Aunt Kate. And Bess has a good time."

"Bring Bess to the dance. She'll have a good time there. Plenty of people bring their kids."

"With all that noise and liquor? And middle-aged men out in the parking lot knocking each other down and vomiting on their running boards? What kind of people take children to that?"

"My kind."

"You don't have a kind, Archer. You're an only one."

The time she said that, he pushed her down hard. Bess had been in her room, but she had heard Celia fall against a dining room chair, knocking it over.

Though Celia wore a housedress to the concert, without fail it was a freshly washed and ironed one that smelled of summer mornings on the clothesline. And it was one with a pretty, gathered pocket or a collar she'd trimmed with a bit of lace edging Aunt Kate had tatted. Sometimes she tucked a small bow in her hair. And her arms and cheeks smelled of lily of the valley.

Often Donna's family came, too, so the two little girls could skip off to the popcorn stand by themselves, then stroll among the many blankets, pretending to be grown-up women discussing their husbands and children.

"My husband is so kind, he never yells at me or Marilyn." Marilyn was Bess's imaginary daughter, who started piano lessons when she was two. "He makes two hundred dollars a month, and he gives almost all of it to me. He takes me to the pictures once a week, and he sings and claps when Marilyn plays the piano."

"My husband is crabby," Donna lamented. "And sometimes he gets drunk and yells at me and hits me. And he spanks little Darlene. And we don't have much money, and if he doesn't get nicer, I'm going to go stay at my aunt's." Then she would add importantly, "Isn't it a shame?"

Before the band struck up the concluding "God Bless America," Bess and Donna slipped away from the park, wandering uptown to see if the first showing of *The Quiet Man* had let out.

Main Street was nearly empty. Constable Wall's car sat in front of Anderson's Candy and Ice Cream; a few other cars were lined up in front of the Majestic. The movie wouldn't let out, said the little clock in the cashier's booth, for fifteen minutes.

"I don't want to hang around waiting like I'm a pick-up," Donna said. "Let's walk down to the Lucky."

A couple of cars drove slowly by, one filled with boys from Ula who honked and whistled, the other with three college girls, Beverly Ridza and a couple of her friends, with whom Bess and Donna were acquainted from a respectful distance. Was it possible that in two years Bess and Donna would themselves be as smooth and evolved as the girls in the car?

"I'm glad we didn't stand around waiting in front of the Majestic," said Donna, who was sensitive about being without a steady boyfriend this summer. "It makes you look desperate."

Bess didn't feel desperate. She felt . . . expectant, as if she were waiting for a package in the mail.

In a few weeks she was going to St. Cloud Teachers College, less than two hundred miles away, a place unlikely to hold a lot of surprises. Still, it was the first step toward something far away and high up, something she would have to stretch to reach. She didn't know what, only that when she reached it, it would grab her roughly and pull her along, and she would welcome it.

She didn't want to be a teacher, but Aunt Kate, who'd taught, always said, "Get the certificate anyway. You never know when you might need it." Bess wasn't sure she approved of that. It seemed cowardly and awfully bourgeois, but she would do it just to please her aunt, since teaching was what Celia had planned to do before she met Archer. Getting the certificate would ease some longing in Kate, and after she had it, Bess would fly out into the world and find her own fortune.

When she had a fortune, she would ask Aunt Kate to come live with her. If Kate wanted to stay in her own house, Bess would buy her what she needed and hire a cleaning woman.

Earning your own money was best. Bess might marry a rich husband, but she wouldn't need his money. Aunt Kate had always said, "If you marry for money, you'll work hard for your wages." Not that anyone in the family had ever had the opportunity to marry for money.

Aunt Kate also said, "Marry in haste, repent at leisure." Too bad Celia hadn't listened to that. Kate had, as well, a number of strictures regarding what *not* to wear to be married. "Marry in black, wish yourself back" was one. "Marry in red, wish yourself dead" was another. But who would marry in black or red? Pearls were bad luck. "They're tears," Kate said. "The more you wear, the more you'll shed." Celia had worn simulated pearls when she was married.

The old Harvester Arms Hotel, down by the railroad tracks, fronted onto Main Street, but you went around to the south side, facing the tracks, and down a flight of iron steps to enter the bar. Bess liked the Lucky Club. It inspired small and pleasant expectations, as if truly it might be lucky.

The booths were unpadded pine. Beer signs covered the smoke-darkened wood-paneled walls, a couple of them electric, one with a waterfall that tumbled and frothed, another with foam rising in a pilsner glass and spilling carelessly over the sides. Nobody in Harvester owned a pilsner glass. Well, maybe Mr. Albers the lawyer. He thought he was pretty grand.

Half a dozen customers sat in booths and at the horseshoe-shaped bar as Bess and Donna slid into the third booth. Hammy Kretzmarsky called from behind the bar, "What'll you ladies have?"

"Two Millers," Donna called back.

Hammy was, everyone agreed, a helluva nice guy. He was young, good-looking, and bright, so why had he buried himself here, beneath the Harvester Arms, running a three-two joint? In a spot on the road like Harvester, where everyone knew everything about everyone else, one thing they didn't know was why Hammy stuck around.

Some said he had lost heart when his young wife left him for a wealthy car dealer from Sioux Falls, South Dakota, but Hammy was always sunny and full of stories and harmless gossip. Others said he was socking away money to buy a real bar in Minneapolis, but could you sock away money in the three-two business? Still others said he was writing a book about World War II. He'd been a marine in the South Pacific.

But if Hammy was writing a book, no one ever heard him mention it, and no one asked. You didn't ask Hammy personal questions, no matter how many evenings you whiled away with him in the Lucky Club.

Bess thought maybe Hammy had a secret lover, possibly a chippy from the south side of town. There weren't many of those. One or two. Most lit out for Sioux Falls or the Twin Cities, but occasionally an easy girl came along, without fear or ambition, who stuck around to provoke people. Maybe Hammy was seeing that kind of girl, though Bess didn't see how it could be kept a secret. Most secrets in Harvester were well known.

But Hammy remained a mystery. Such mysteries, such dark knots in the thread of things, prevented people from going mad from boredom in villages.

One of the six other customers in the Lucky was a boy in army uniform with a corporal's stripes, no one Bess or Donna knew. From one of the little towns around Harvester, Ula or Red Berry or some other such place.

The boy was with another who looked to be a farmer, very sunburned up to a line where his work cap shaded him. Above the line the skin was pale as a kitchen sink. The two were doubtless brothers, both with pale eyes and long thin noses.

The soldier fed coins into the jukebox, and he and his

brother punched buttons. The first song was "Laura," played by Stan Kenton's band.

Hitching up their belts with self-conscious nonchalance, the corporal and his brother strolled over to Bess and Donna's booth. "Dance?" the brother asked Donna, and the soldier held out his hand to Bess.

branches. Pink cheeked and blowzy, they were, like that good-natured hired girl who'd worked for Clara and Chauncey long ago. Bobbing vacuously in the least breeze, the flowers looked slightly simple, but Kate was fond of them, as she had been of the girl whom they all knew to be generous with her favors.

Reaching the back stoop, Kate grasped the trellis again, steadying herself as she climbed the steps. At the top, she rested, shifting her weight and massaging her tender left hip with her free hand. She was a bit weak and nauseated tonight. The "Way Back When" piece lay like something sour and undigested in her middle.

Ten years ago she had been forty-nine—"still a young woman," Frieda would say—and her husband, Martin, had been dead only eight months. The two deaths, Martin's and Celia's, one following so closely on the other, had ripped her roots right out of the ground.

Death had shadowed Kate since 1917, when her older sister, Clara, and Clara's husband, Chauncey, had both died of influenza, leaving behind a lovely baby. Celia. Childless, Kate and Martin had adopted the infant, embracing her with love so profound it surprised them.

What a magical child Celia had been. So pretty and bright. Cheerful and kind and helpful as well. Born to be a teacher, Kate had always said. When she was only three, Celia had begged to wipe dishes! With infinite delicacy she had held a saucer, caressing it with the towel until it was dry, then laying it on the seat of a kitchen chair. Think of it.

Until she met that Okie, Celia had never given Kate

and Martin a moment's worry. A day didn't pass, even now, ten years after the accident, when Kate didn't ask, "Why? What did she see in him?"

To give the devil his due, Archer had been handsome. And he had had a bad arm. A sensitive, soft-hearted girl might be drawn by his infirmity, imagining that she could make up for it. No, it hadn't been that simple. He had been a disease, and Celia had fallen sick with need of him.

Kate whacked at the nearest mock orange bush with her cane, then winced as pain shot out from her wrist and elbow and shoulder. Steadying herself against the trellis, she saw the August night in 1942 settling around her, visible and ghostly.

There on the steps was Celia, dressed in a plain, mauve cotton shift, wearing a single strand of simulated pearls and white pumps that she'd borrowed money to have resoled. Her short dark hair fluffed around her face as if spun from something very fine, and she looked seventeen and innocent again. She held seven-year-old Bess's hand.

"It's all right, then, if she stays all night?" Celia had asked, bending to kiss Bess. If Archer drank himself blind and kept them out till dawn, she didn't want Kate to know.

"Of course."

"Send her home after breakfast." She leaned to kiss Kate's cheek, but Archer had honked, not once but several harsh brays, startling Celia so that she grew flustered and backed away, waving.

Such an incomplete, unsatisfactory good-bye. Kate held her hand outstretched toward the vision, but dropped it suddenly, heaving a rough sigh as it evaporated.

God had forgiven the world the death of His son. Well, she wasn't God. She was a spiteful old woman, and Archer had been a willful, driven fool. She hoped he was rotting in hell.

And Archer's child was willful, too. Bess was clever and unforgetting and willful. And she could not tolerate disaffection, not even the possibility. She must always be the one who forsook. She would half bury you under her affection and generosity, but let there be a hint of disloyalty or retreat on your part, and she'd pull back as from a leper, walking away without a backward glance. Look how she'd treated Mrs. Stubbs, the piano teacher.

Opening the back screen door and flicking on the porch light, in the event that Harriet or Bess came in that way, Kate headed toward the dim, distant living room and her rocking chair.

Whom did Bess trust? Kate wondered, the trail of thought winding onward down the same path. Kate, Donna, and Harriet. Perhaps that was all.

Harriet had been awfully good to the child after Celia's death, clucking over her, giving her her first bicycle, taking her to the movies and on trips to the Cities. She'd shared her time and money as if Bess were her own.

Now Harriet deserved a splash of romance, though Kate doubted there'd be much of that in an alliance with DeVore Weiss. But if marriage to DeVore didn't bring Harriet romance, it would at least bring her the kiss of conventional domesticity, a condition for which she sorely longed. Harriet felt a great hungering to say "my house" and "my husband," a need not to live on the edge of someone else's life. And Harriet would more than keep up her end of the bargain. She always gave more than she got, for fear of stinting. No, DeVore Weiss would have no reason to regret marrying Harriet, should he be so wise.

Easing herself into the rocker, Kate thought: Bess has to see how much she owes Harriet. It would be too bad if Harriet were to lose Bess. Harriet's world was meager to begin with, while Bess's world was expanding, opening like gates swung wide. After Labor Day she would be gone. Off to college. Off to the world.

She gripped the arm of the rocker as though clinging to a safe place. She guessed that she loved Bess even more than she had loved Celia. Loving Celia had been as effortless as breathing, while loving Bess was often aggravating. But once you'd invested your wit and effort, you created something larger and stronger than what could be had without labor or tears.

Losing Harriet, if she married DeVore Weiss, would be hard enough for Kate, though Harriet would move only a few miles, out to the Weiss farm. Bess's departure, on the other hand, was a double loss: not only the child gone but, with her, the last tangible remnant of Celia.

Nevertheless, Kate was desperate to see Bess away. Harvester, for Bess, was a stifling, cramped room too full of old photographs, fading yet potent reminders of scandal and exclusion. If she stayed, the lingering must of disgrace would undo her. And she would go bad.

Kate nodded her head emphatically. College was needed. And that thought reminded her: Anthea Dorsey had phoned for Bess, and Kate had forgotten to mention it. Anthea was inviting a few college-bound friends out to Sioux Woman Lake to the Dorseys' cottage for a Sunday-afternoon party.

Kate pressed the cane hard against the floor and set the rocker moving. A few months after Celia's death that same Anthea, seven then, had issued party invitations. Bess had come home from school excited because she was going to Anthea's birthday party.

"Where's the invitation?" Kate asked. "When's the party?"

"I don't know, but all the girls in the class are going to be invited."

"Well, when she gives you your invitation, bring it home and we'll buy a present."

The following day Kate asked if Anthea had passed out the invitations.

"Yes," Bess told her.

"And where is yours?"

"Anthea forgot it or it got lost or something, 'cause when she got to school, she didn't have it."

Bess was sitting at the dining room table with her schoolbooks and papers. Kate sat down opposite.

"If Anthea doesn't invite you—"

"She's going to! She said she was going to. I believe her! Don't say she's not!"

"Listen to me. I'm not saying that—but if she doesn't, it won't have anything to do with how nice you are. You're the nicest girl in the second grade, whether you get an invitation or not."

The invitation had not been forthcoming. Rightly, Bess

blamed Mrs. Dorsey, not Anthea, but the harm had been done. The child felt accused of something, without knowing what it was.

"Chk, chk, chk." Muttering meaningless syllables of exasperation, Kate struggled to let go of her thoughts, to let go of the hatred of Archer Canby that burned in her joints and shriveled her body. Beside her, stacked on the living room radiator, were copies of *Country Gentleman*. Still muttering, she shook her head and reached for the September issue, which had arrived yesterday.

Then the phone was ringing. They'd have to hold on until she could get there. Her hip would not carry her quickly. *I'm coming. I'm coming. Keep ringing.*

"Hello?"

"Kate. Frieda. Can you walk across the street for cards?"

"Yes."

"Harriet's not home?"

"She's with Rose Miller tonight."

"Then I'll call Marie Wall for a fourth."

When she'd returned the receiver to the cradle, Kate sat for some minutes marveling at how the world turned around, and how the day turned around, and how she could be brooding and pessimistic one minute and then have the gray wiped away as if it were finger marks on the woodwork by something like Frieda's homely voice coming too loud over the wire. Frieda still talked on the phone as though she were a country girl calling to town on an echoing, crackling six-party line.

What card game would they play, Kate wondered,

bridge or Five Hundred? Frieda wasn't much good at contract bridge, and Kate wasn't so fond of auction bridge. But it didn't matter, it didn't matter.

With one hand on her cane and the other on the desk where Celia's picture smiled at her, she prised herself up and started off to Frieda's.

CHAPTER 7

Harriet

"How soon should we leave for the dance?" Rose Miller asked.

Harriet glanced at the electric clock on her friend's stove. "It's almost eight. I guess we can leave any time we're finished here."

The two women were clearing supper dishes in the kitchen of Rose's apartment, down the street from the public library. Harvester had only two structures that might be called apartment buildings. This, the Ashley Building, was one of them. It had fourteen units, four on each of three floors, and two in the basement. Rose had one of the basement units. The basement apartments rented for less.

Harriet didn't think she would ever want to live in a basement apartment. She didn't like the idea of people walking by outside, looking down on her. She also didn't like the idea of looking *up* to see out. If a woman were walking past on the sidewalk, you could see her underslip. Harriet herself felt uncomfortable walking by the Ashley Building, even though she knew the two basement apartments were rented to women, Rose and Mrs. Harvey.

On the other hand, the basement units were heavenly cool in summer and cozy in winter. The nice thing about the Ashley Building, if you were single, was that it was right in the heart of things, near the library, half a block from the school, and less than a block from Main Street. Of course, if you were married and especially if you had children, you wouldn't want to be this close to Main Street. The children would always be wandering off. Harriet put thoughts of children from her mind. One thing at a time. Dreaming too far ahead was bad luck.

"The chicken salad was delicious," she told Rose. "I'm glad you didn't put in onion," she added, thinking of the dance ahead.

"It was my mother's recipe, rest her soul." Rose lowered their two plates and silverware into sudsy water.

"Could I have it or don't you like to give it out?"

"The recipe? Sure. I'll copy it down before we leave."

Harriet put on the apron Rose handed her and picked up a dish towel. She felt fluttery and slightly nauseated. No fault of the chicken salad. The salad had been fine—not as good as what *she* made, but fine. She'd asked for the recipe because it made Rose feel good, and it was one of those things that women did, especially married women.

No, she felt this kind of sickening before all the dances at the Dakota since that first time DeVore Weiss had asked her to fill out a threesome for the butterfly. Rose didn't understand what Harriet saw in DeVore. She wasn't sure she understood it herself. He was a long drink of water, with face and hands a cordovan color from the sun. He had hawkish features and only one, all-purpose and indecipherable, expression. Whatever energies would have gone into facial expression, he saved for farming and dancing.

And fathering children. His wife had given him six before she was carried off by sleeping sickness. Two of the children were grown: DeVore Junior, who had moved to Worthington, the Turkey Capital of the World, where he had some connection with the turkey business, and Daryl, who lived in Harvester and worked at the Chevrolet garage.

Although he had two children grown and gone from the farm, DeVore was only forty-two. He was not some old man who was only looking for a cook and cleaning woman. He loved to dance and he told her he liked movies, although he hadn't asked her to one. Actually, he hadn't asked her to anything. But of course his wife was less than a year in the ground, and Harriet would have felt improper parading to the movies with him so soon. But it would be nice if he asked to take her home from the dance one of these nights. She didn't think that would be too disrespectful.

She and Rose had made an agreement that if one of them got asked home from the dance, the other would drive the car home, whether it was Rose's or Harriet's.

"What if someone asked to take you home from the dance," Harriet began, drying spoons and forks and returning them to their spaces in the drawer, "and someone also asked me? Who would drive the car home?"

Rose rinsed an iced-tea glass and set it in the drainer, then wrung water from the dishcloth and began to wipe off the counter and the kitchen table. She was thinking.

"We could leave the car there and one of us drive the other back to get it the next day."

"Of course. That's a wonderful idea."

Relieved, Harriet resumed her thoughts of DeVore. DeVore was three years older than Harriet. It was right that a man should be older than his wife—not that Harriet was saying she was going to be his wife. But she was glad she was younger.

It had been—what was that word?—*kismet*, the way they'd met. Harriet didn't usually go to Old Time night. The music was, well, common. But that night she and Rose had been to see *The African Queen* at the Majestic, and when it let out, they were both restless and not ready to go home.

In all honesty, the movie may have had some effect on them, since Katharine Hepburn played a woman who was no longer a spring chicken, but who nevertheless found true love with Humphrey Bogart, who was not exactly a strapping boy either.

In any case, Rose had said impulsively, "Let's go see who's at the Dakota."

Harriet wasn't sure. They stood huddled under the marquee, a frigid April wind slapping their calves and reaching up their skirts.

Rose looked at her watch. "It'll be after ten when we get there. At Old Time everybody's in free after ten." Pulling her collar up, she whined, "I'm freezing. For the love of Mike, let's go *someplace*."

That was how Harriet happened to be at the Dakota on a Wednesday night. Well, actually, DeVore went to the modern dances on the weekends as well, but Harriet thought he might not have asked her to dance if he hadn't been looking for a third for the butterfly, and of course that could only happen on a Wednesday.

She didn't know how it was that they'd hit it off so well right away. They had almost nothing in common. Harriet had never lived on a farm, and DeVore had never lived in town. Harriet was a business-school graduate, and DeVore had quit high school in the eleventh grade, when his dad had been hurt in an accident with the combine.

DeVore liked any music with a hard beat that made the floor shake, whereas Harriet collected love songs and semiclassical records. She was partial to Carmen Cavallero, André Kostelanetz, and Phil Spitalny and His All Girl Orchestra.

Harriet was at the library once a week checking out Taylor Caldwell and Edna Ferber and Howard Fast. Upon tactful cross-examination, DeVore confessed to having no time for reading beyond the *Standard Ledger*, and sometimes he fell asleep before he finished that.

Still, they found things to talk about: the weather, the farm, Harriet's work at the Water and Power Company, the latest John Wayne movie. She had shown an interest in all things agricultural, and he now felt comfortable sharing with her the problems he was having with a couple of milk cows.

As their friendship grew more secure, Harriet determined not to throw herself at him. The man was still in mourning, for one thing. And she was a romantic who believed that man should pursue and woman flee. Well, perhaps not *flee*, literally, but not fall all over him, at any rate. Besides, she wasn't that desperate. She'd had chances. Not proposals, exactly, but interested men who would have proposed, she didn't doubt, had fate not intervened.

Herb Brilley, who used to work at the Water and Power Company, had been interested. Hadn't they dated for several months before he'd inherited a piece of land in Oregon and thrown over his position? And Bill Hahn. They'd been close before he landed that high-paying job in Greenland that he would have been a fool to turn down. For that matter, quite possibly Bill Hahn would show up one of these days looking for her.

No, Harriet wasn't desperate, and she wasn't about to give DeVore that impression. Nothing made a man run faster than a desperate-seeming woman. At the same time, she felt that she was definitely ready for marriage. She wasn't some fool girl who would let the dishes pile up in the sink or the dirty clothes molder in the laundry basket. She was trained and ripened and ready to run a household. Not for nothing had she clipped articles from *Better Homes and Gardens* every month. She would come to DeVore laden with information regarding inexpensive home beautification and repairs, as well as delicious seasonal recipes.

Also, unlike young girls, Harriet had had a career. She'd had the experience of making her own way in the world. She was not unprepared to give that up, of course, but she wouldn't find herself standing at DeVore's washing machine, yearning for what might have been.

If, on the other hand, DeVore wanted her to continue

working at the Water and Power Company until the children were raised, she was prepared to do that. It would mean having less time for sewing slipcovers and embroidering pillow slips, but a mature woman understood the necessity of sacrifice.

"I suppose you'll be looking for DeVore Weiss," Rose said as she turned the Chevrolet onto Second Street and drove west toward the highway.

"If he's there, I'll probably have a dance or two with him."

They could hear the high school band in the park playing "Bali Hai." Not a tune that showed them off to advantage.

"You want to stop at the band concert before we go to the Dakota?" Rose asked. "It's still early. You used to love the band concerts."

"No. Let's get to the dance." *I used to love the band concerts, that's true. I didn't have this awful, anxious feeling then, this fear of seeing him and fear of not.*

She closed her eyes and tried to breathe deeply, but there didn't seem to be room enough down there in her lungs.

CHAPTER 8

Bess

"You're just home on leave?" Bess asked the soldier, whose name was Jim Arliss.

"Yeah. I wish I was getting out, but that won't be for a while. You finished with high school?"

"I'm going to college in September."

"I wish to hell I was back in high school. I used to hate it. I was in trouble all the time, but I'd sure like to have that kind of trouble again. You like school?"

"It was okay. I'm not going to miss it."

"You would if you was in Korea." He laughed. "If any-body'd told me I was going to miss school, I'da said they was a damned liar. I see now what a good time I was having. Maybe you'll find out you were having a good time and didn't even know it."

"Maybe," she said, unconvinced.

The music ended and they walked the few steps back to the booth.

"OK if Bob and I sit with you and your friend awhile?"

"Sure." Bess knew that nothing was going to come of it. He was a nice boy who'd probably dreamed about coming home on leave and, now that he was home, didn't know what to do with himself. Life had gone on while he was away; things had changed. He wanted someone to help him kill time until he went back to the army, where things hadn't changed while he was away.

The four of them, she and Donna, Jim and Bob, sat drinking beer and talking about things Bess had no interest in. But you wouldn't walk away from a boy home on leave. You didn't have to neck with him or anything, but you wouldn't hurt his feelings. What if he went back to Korea and was killed?

They talked about cars, stock cars in particular. When Jim got out of the service, he and Bob planned to break into stock car racing. Bob was an ace mechanic, and Jim could drive the hell out of anything on wheels.

Bess knew little about cars. She'd taken driver's education in school, and she had her license, but her aunt didn't own a car. Harriet had a perfectly maintained 1940 Ford sedan, but she didn't like other people driving it, so Bess was rarely behind the wheel and had nothing to contribute to the moment's conversation beyond "Really?" Donna, too, was out of her depth. But she had slipped into one of her film roles—Jane Powell in *Small Town Girl*, maybe—and giggled and asked all sorts of foolish questions, which Jim and Bob were tickled to answer.

Bess excused herself and went to the restroom to reapply her lipstick. She and Donna should leave soon. The longer they stayed, the more serious would be the Arliss boys' expectations. She'd hoped Donna would follow her to the restroom to discuss this, but Donna was ankle deep in valves and ratios.

Two other fellows had joined the group in the booth

when Bess came out of the restroom. The one seated and facing her direction was Earl Ingbretson of Ingbretson's Hatchery. The second, standing and leaning against the side of the booth, had his back to her. When men saw a uniform, they collected around it. Bess wasn't sure why that was. To pay tribute? To suffer the war experience again or vicariously? Earl Ingbretson had been in World War II.

Bess ordered another Miller from Hammy and sat down close by at the bar.

"Did we crowd you out?" the second newcomer asked, noticing her at the bar. It was Doyle Hanlon. She only knew him by name. He was a lot older, maybe twenty-five or so.

"It doesn't matter. I'm fine. Anyway, it's cooler here."

Hammy brought beers for Earl and Doyle, and the Arlisses ordered another round for themselves and Donna. The evening was getting bogged down. Bess didn't want to talk about war and cars. She wanted to sneak out and walk home, but Donna would have a fit.

Doyle Hanlon and Earl Ingbretson were both married. Their wives had probably gone to the band concert. Or maybe they belonged to a ladies' bowling league over in St. Bridget. Or maybe they were home in front of the electric fan, ironing dress shirts for their husbands and putting the kids to bed.

Husbands in Harvester came out for beer or a ball game without their wives. No one thought anything of it, except maybe the wives. Bess knew that young, newly married men were teased by their friends if they gave up going out with the boys. Henpecked. In Harvester a young man could be out with his friends three or four nights a week without his wife having an excuse to give him hell. If Bess were one of those wives, she'd give him hell anyway.

When the ball game ended, eight or ten fans drifted into the Lucky Club. The Harvester Blue Jays had lost to the Red Berry Red Sox, six to eight. No one was dispirited. The games were fun but they weren't serious. The new arrivals ordered beers and slipped quarters into the jukebox. Bess glanced at her watch. Ten o'clock. The evening was three weeks long already and she couldn't catch Donna's eye.

"Would you like to dance?" Doyle Hanlon asked.

"I might as well," she said, leading the way to the tiny dance floor.

"Sorry if Earl and I horned in on your date."

"I don't have a date. Donna and I came by for a beer after the band concert."

"Earl saw the uniform and wanted to say hello to the kid."

"Were you in the service?"

"Briefly." He smiled. "I even enlisted. Had a crazy idea I needed the shit kicked out of me before I'd be a man. It's not true, as rumored, that I shot myself in the foot to get out," he assured her, still smiling. "I got drunk one night and flipped a motorcycle outside of Pusan. It only hurts when it rains," he said, letting go of Bess's hand to pat his left thigh. "I think the limp's distinguished, don't you?"

"I didn't notice that you had a limp."

Smoothly, for a man with a limp, Doyle Hanlon spun

her around and dipped deeply as the song ended. Bess had no trouble following his steps. For that she was grateful to Harriet.

When Bess was in the eighth grade, Harriet had bought dance records—fox-trots and waltzes and Latin rhythms—at Mather's Five and Dime, then rolled up the dining room rug and sprinkled talcum powder on the floor. A good dancer with a knack for leading, Harriet waltzed Bess around the dining room several hundred times as her portable phonograph played "You're Breaking My Heart."

Now Bess and Doyle Hanlon stood by the jukebox waiting for another waltz, this one "Remember" by Irving Berlin.

"You work at the Loon Cafe, don't you?"

"Right."

"What's your name?"

"Bess Canby."

"Oh, yes."

Did that mean, "Oh, yes, you're Archer Canby's kid. He got drunk and piled up his car back when I was in high school"? Maybe Doyle Hanlon had been driving home after a date that night. Maybe he'd seen Archer's Ford wrapped around the cottonwood.

He said, "I saw an article by you in the *Standard Ledger* a couple of months back. There was a picture of you. I don't remember what it was about."

"Trying to get businessmen to donate money for new band uniforms."

"That's right. I mentioned it to my dad and we sent a check."

"What exactly does your dad do?" She knew where his office was, above the *Standard Ledger*, but not what went on there.

When the song ended, they stood waiting for yet another. "The old man inherited money. Not millions, just what was left after the Crash. They were from St. Louis, my dad's people. His old man jumped out of a window on Pine Street in downtown St. Louis. His uncle took a short swim across a wide river."

"Oh, dear. I'm sorry."

"I don't remember either of them. I was two years old at the time, three when we came here. Dad had an old buddy up this way who was buying up foreclosed farms from banks. The old man bought a bunch of 'em and rented some of them back to the original owners—not a popular business. Then he started buying and selling cattle and raising purebreds on the side. But what he likes best is dabbling in futures. He's a lucky SOB, made a small bundle at it."

"Dabbling in futures? What's that?"

"Oh boy."

"Oh boy?"

"It's hard explaining commodities futures."

"Try. I'm smart."

"Well, when you buy futures, you're buying something that hasn't been produced or harvested yet, and you're gambling that it's going to go up in price."

"For instance?"

"Corn. Wheat. Hogs. Things like that."

"A lot can affect those. Weather, for one thing."

"That's what makes dabbling in futures such a dangerous game. It's not for boys."

"Your dad must like it."

"He's a tough son of a bitch."

Bess thought of the office on the second floor of the *Standard Ledger*. She'd never been up there, but she'd seen the gold lettering on the bay window all her life. HANLON LAND AND INVESTMENTS. The words were printed in thick, heavy-looking gold letters, as if matters of considerable import were carried on behind them. She imagined Oriental carpets on the floor, mahogany desks, leather-covered chairs. Maybe a leather sofa where the senior Hanlon stretched out in the late afternoon before descending the wide stairway to the street.

The senior Hanlon, a slender, upright gentleman, didn't come into the Loon Cafe, but Bess saw him on Main Street occasionally. More elegant in his attire than other men in Harvester, he always wore expensive three-piece suits and, invariably, a hat, usually a gray fedora in cold weather, a fresh-looking panama in summer. He was one of only three men in town who wore cream-colored suits in hot weather.

"And what do *you* do?" Bess asked Doyle Hanlon.

"I work for the old man. I keep his books, take care of his taxes, and oversee the farms."

"He still has the farms he bought during the Depression?"

"Oh yes. He's never mortgaged the farms to play with futures. He'll gamble with anything, except what he calls 'home base.'"

Bess thought that she could listen to a great deal more

about the Hanlons. Was that because they were fascinating or because something about Doyle made what he said seem extraordinary? How had she lived seventeen years in Harvester and never had a conversation with him before? Well, of course, she had been a child most of those years.

"Have you dabbled in futures?"

"Only once or twice when something looked especially good. It'd be awfully easy to get hooked. The old man's seen plenty of men wiped out. Anyway, I don't have a lot of capital to play with, so I'm pretty selective."

"Why doesn't your dad tell you which ones to buy?"

Doyle Hanlon frowned. After a long moment he said, "I went to Korea to become my own man."

The younger Hanlon looked nothing like his father. Though slender like Herbert Hanlon, he was only about five-eight. Bess was nearly as tall. His skin was olive and his hair the color of a tarnished penny. Herbert Hanlon, on the other hand, must once have had black hair since his bony face was dominated by prickly thickets of sooty brow, though the thatch on his head was now electric white.

Where the senior Hanlon's eyes were ice blue and seemed oblivious to who or what was immediately before him, Doyle's eyes were mahogany brown and took in everything, finding it all amusing. The skin at their corners creased, and his mouth persistently curled in a wry half smile.

His amusement intrigued Bess. She wished she could see the world from inside his head. What did it look like? His private world was exotic compared with hers. His grandfather and great-uncle had both committed suicide over lost fortunes. His father dabbled in futures. All her life she'd heard grain and livestock futures quoted on the radio, without any notion of what they were. Now that she knew, they seemed enthralling.

Why hadn't her father been like Doyle Hanlon's, someone who made money instead of trouble? Well, she'd loved Archer, if it came to that. When you were little, you didn't know how *not* to love your father. She didn't love him now. She knew too much.

Celia had been too damned Christian to walk away from Archer or too crazy about him. And the teacher in Celia had imagined that Archer was educable, that he could learn peace and patience from her example. Whatever he did, she forgave him, and her forgiveness drove him crazy.

Bess now thought that he had wanted to be despised. He'd wanted Celia to get drunk and throw things at him, wanted to subdue and humble her at the height of her rage. He had wanted her to loathe him for his crippled arm, and then he wanted to punish her for her loathing. Like something out of Dostoyevsky. That was his way of loving her. Insane, but it was his way.

Poor Celia had been incapable of cooperating. That sort of cooperation was something that she would not even have grasped. Bess recalled times when Archer had seemed ready to kill her mother for not loathing him, for not cooperating in his needs.

But two weeks before the accident, Celia's patience had run out. Or so Bess had thought. Aunt Kate did not know that, and Bess would never tell her. If she knew how miserable Celia had been in the last days, Kate would never have a moment's peace.

Over Doyle Hanlon's shoulder, Bess stared into the turquoise-blue streaks of the rainbow on the front of the jukebox. Celia had worn a turquoise-blue dress occasionally, a summer cotton dress with a deep square neck that she'd run up on Aunt Kate's old Singer.

She'd worn that dress to Methodist Ladies' Aid Circle one summer afternoon two weeks before the accident. The Circle had met in the church basement that day because the women were sorting clothes for the September rummage sale.

Bess and Donna had come along with their mothers, and Celia had settled them at a table in the Sunday school area, each girl with a pair of round-tipped scissors for cutting out paper dolls.

By midafternoon Bess had cut out all the gowns for her Ginger Rogers doll, and Donna had lined up the paper wardrobe for Betty Grable. As they were getting down to serious play, Donna had said, "I gotta go to the bathroom. Come with."

"No." Bess fastened a slinky gold frock to Ginger's shoulders.

"Why?"

"'Cuz. It stinks in there like mothballs. It's the stuff they put in the toilet. You better go before you wet your pants."

A moment later Donna was back. "Mommy won't let me in. What'll I do?"

"Well, go in the men's."

"The *men's*?"

"You want to wet your pants?"

"What if a man comes in?"

"*What* man?"

In the end Bess had had to go with Donna into the men's room. When they came out, they stood for several minutes outside the women's with their ears pressed against the door.

Celia and Donna's mother were on the other side, their voices muffled. Celia was crying and Florence kept saying, "It's gossip, old gossip."

Bess began pounding on the door.

"You shouldn't do that," Donna told her. "They'll get mad. Come on." She tugged at Bess.

But Bess continued, crying, "Let me in, Mommy. What's wrong? Let me in!"

Florence Olson opened the door. "Shhhh," she shushed Bess, putting a finger to her lips. "Your mommy's feeling a little sick, Bess. She'll be okay. Go get your paper dolls, both of you. We're going home now. Don't say anything to the other women."

Inside the disinfectant-reeking bathroom, Bess could see her mother hunched into a corner, staring straight ahead and weeping, her face sort of broken into pieces. Bess tried to push past Donna's mother, but Florence was firm. "If you want to help your mommy, get your paper dolls and go out to the car and wait."

The rest of that afternoon Celia and Florence bent their heads together in the Olson living room, sighing and murmuring in pale, painful shades of conversation, while Bess and Donna sat glumly speculating in the backyard. Once the girls crept around to crouch beneath the open living room windows, listening to words they didn't understand, at least not then.

"Her name was Millie Jessup. Don't you remember, Flo? She graduated with *us*." Celia's voice was weak, as if she'd said the same things over and over and was tired and even bored, but with a boredom that weighed about a thousand pounds.

"I thought she died of a ruptured appendix. Someone told me that." Again and again the words "ruptured appendix" came into the conversation. Then, in a shudder, "She *bled* to death, Flo."

After a reverberant pause, "Archer was hired man for the Jessups."

"That doesn't mean anything," Florence told her.

"Yes, it does. Meredith Smitt said he sent the girl to a butcher in Sioux Falls."

A butcher, Bess pondered. Why would you send a girl to a butcher?

Bess had been made to stay for dinner at Donna's, while her mother went home. She had no appetite although Florence had fried up a chicken and made mashed potatoes and corn on the cob. Bess tried not to play with her food, but she couldn't stop wondering what a butcher in Sioux Falls had to do with a girl's bleeding to death. And even if Archer *had* told the girl to go to the butcher, how did that make him to blame? It didn't make sense.

Bess knew that while she sat at the Olsons' kitchen table, Celia was talking to Archer about Millie Jessup. What was

Archer saying? At one point Bess thought she heard her father shout, "Ten years!" Despite the heat, Florence got up and closed the kitchen window.

After dinner Florence sent the girls into the living room to listen to the radio with Hy Olson. But Mr. Olson turned the dial to war news, so Donna got out the playing cards. Bess didn't feel like playing rummy, and after a couple of hands she'd put her head down on the Axminster carpet and fallen asleep.

When she woke, Bess thought at first that she'd slept all night on the Olsons' floor. Hours seemed to have passed. But Hy Olson was still listening to the radio.

Bess's cheek was sweaty and chapped from the rug, and her hair was sticking to the damp skin. Crusted sleep prickled in the corners of her eyes, her ears buzzed, and she was having trouble thinking straight. She wanted to go back to sleep, but Celia was there, waking her, being cross, holding her hand and pulling her to her feet.

"She can stay here," Florence offered.

"No."

Celia was weeping in front of Hy Olson. Even in her daze, Bess found that alarming. Staggering, she strove to keep up as her mother pulled her out the front door and down the steps, while Florence Olson stood in the doorway looking helpless and calling, "Telephone me tomorrow."

Bess was fully awake now as they waited beneath a streetlight for a car to pass. Her mother continued to weep soundlessly as if she might never stop. Would the people in the car see Celia crying? A sense of doom crept over Bess. If your mother cried in the street, the future was not safe.

They heard Archer behind them, calling for them to wait. There was liquor in his voice and, worse, tears. Bess tried to pull away from her mother and run to Aunt Kate's. She didn't want to be part of this spectacle. Celia held Bess's hand in a painful grip, forgetting entirely that the child was there.

Archer, smelling of bourbon and breathing hard from his run, grabbed Celia's arm, pulling at her roughly.

"Come home," he demanded.

"No."

"There's more I have to say. Things I didn't tell you."

"No."

"What's going to happen?"

"I don't know. Let me go now."

"You're taking Bess?"

"Did you think I'd leave her with *you*?"

Celia reeled as he swung the back of his hand across her face. She stepped off the curb, pulling Bess with her.

Archer stood on the spot, yelling after them, "Goddamn you, go then. Fucking bitch."

Inside their open-windowed houses, people could hear Archer, could see them all under the streetlight. Trying to shut out the sound of Archer's yelling, Bess huddled against her mother as they stepped along, holding tightly to each other's hands the rest of the way.

The neighbors had probably shaken their heads, Bess now reflected. On the street they probably eyed Archer askance for his brutality and drunkenness. But no one said anything to him, and what they spoke to one another was by way of oblique and fragmentary references, uttered in half voices on the post office steps, or in the back booth of the Loon Cafe.

More often, Bess imagined, a cocked eyebrow or a referentially lifted shoulder was the slim, self-conscious noting of something amiss but private. One did not confront. To be drunk and abusive to one's wife was a man's private business. Out of self-protection people paid respect to the notion of privacy, even if it was imaginary. If one were to begin preaching and prying, where would it end? Mightn't someone else be preaching and prying into one's *own* life?

Recoiling from the past, Bess was flustered to find that she was clutching Doyle Hanlon's hand.

"Sorry," she said, releasing him and wiping her palm on her skirt.

"I won't run away," he told her and smiled.

How philanthropically he gave his smiles away. They made her feel attractive and clever and like someone else's daughter, not Archer's. And they held Celia at a distance.

Celia had been at Bess's elbow all day, insistent, forcing her way into Bess's thoughts, as if to say, "Pay attention." Giving an impatient shrug to her mother, Bess tried to fix her mind elsewhere. But where? On Doyle's mother, maybe? What was *she* like?

Rebecca Hanlon was wheelchair-bound, Bess knew, though she did not know why. Maybe Doyle would tell her. Mrs. Hanlon was pretty, for a middle-aged woman. Bess had seen her at the Episcopal church bazaars when she'd gone with Aunt Kate and Harriet. The Episcopalians knew how to throw a proper bazaar, Aunt Kate always said. Everything was first-rate and the women still did fine needlework. A little expensive, but worth it.

Despite being an invalid, Mrs. Hanlon was in the thick of things at the bazaars. "Rebecca Hanlon is true royalty," Kate had observed with warm admiration. She'd said nothing about Mr. Hanlon.

About Doyle Hanlon's wife or his twin boys, Bess knew almost nothing, except that his wife's name was Jean and she was tiny and trim and athletic-looking. Her name and picture appeared in the *Standard Ledger* at the end of summer when the paper covered the community tennis tournament. Jean Hanlon was a leading light of that event. Bess had heard that she was from Chicago and that she'd been married to Doyle since both were at Northwestern University, before he'd enlisted in the army.

Bess supposed that Jean, too, was remarkable. Doubtless her father was a surgeon and her mother a symphony cellist. That was the sort of marriage Doyle Hanlon would make.

But it was odd that he'd gone off to Korea, leaving a young wife and children behind. He had enlisted, he said, to get the shit kicked out of him and become a man. Why had he imagined that he wasn't one?

Donna had squeezed out of the booth and crossed the room. "Bess, Jim and Bob are driving over to the Dakota. They said they'd give us a ride over and back if we wanted to go. What d'ya think? It's only ten-thirty. The band plays till one."

Bess had no reason to want to go to the Dakota and no good excuse not to go. She glanced at the Arliss boys, tipping up their bottles and finishing the Millers. They were perfectly fine boys, but she didn't want to be the date of either. If she and Donna were truly just hitching a ride, that was one thing, but . . .

"Let's *all* drive over and see what's happening," Doyle Hanlon suggested as though reading Bess's thoughts. That would make it a party, and no one would be paired with anybody. "Bess, you can ride with Earl and me. Donna can ride with Jim and Bob. Is that all right with you?" he asked Donna.

Bess knew that it was fine with Donna, who, like herself, saw this as having the flavor of a party now. Donna wouldn't feel constrained to kiss either of the Arlisses good night. Although if it came to that, she probably wouldn't mind so much. They were both decent Catholic boys. And Bess and Donna had had nothing but good experiences with Catholic boys.

CHAPTER 9

Harriet

Harriet and Rose had arrived at the Dakota early enough to find a booth near the kitchen. Since this end of the ballroom only smelled of old grease, people dashed to nab one of these booths.

DeVore and his sons Lyle and Delwin had taken a booth two rows over, within hailing distance but not so close as to make Harriet self-conscious. She didn't want to feel herself studied by the two boys. Not that they were in the booth much, except to order beer. They were crazy for dancing, and they cut a daring and athletic path around the floor, cheeks scarlet, eyes fixed, perspiration streaming down their faces.

"God, I've got a thirst," she'd heard Lyle exclaim as he returned to the booth after a wild and wide-ranging polka. The young girl whom he'd honored had looked like someone clinging for life to the back of a runaway horse. "Them polkas take it outta ya."

Harriet had danced four polkas with DeVore. She was very good at the polka, and she was tall so that her steps were well matched to his. She thought it must be difficult for a short woman, like the one he was presently waltzing with, to keep step with a tall man. This woman, a dark-haired, not unattractive divorcée from Ula, by the name of Shirley, barely came to DeVore's shoulder. Shirley's bosom was pressed against him just above his belt buckle.

Men danced with divorcées, but a man with children at home wasn't likely to marry one. Not that there was necessarily anything wrong with a divorcée. She might have been absolutely blameless, married to a brute. That might be the very fact that she was explaining to DeVore now, smiling her injured smile and looking up into his long, bony, believing face.

Here came a fellow from St. Bridget whose name Harriet could never remember. At every dance he asked her several times for waltzes. She didn't think he knew how to polka, and it was just as well because he was a couple of inches shorter than Harriet and it probably wouldn't have worked.

"Harriet, would you care to dance?"

With his hand on her elbow, the St. Bridget fellow—Ernie—led her to the floor, asking after her and what she'd been doing with herself since Sunday, which was when she'd last been to the Dakota.

He wasn't fat. A little stocky. He wore a suit, dress shirt and tie, wing tip shoes and dark socks. He had a good, thick head of hair and a pleasant round face, brown as a nut. He worked for the Highway Department, he'd told her.

He liked his work, especially in winter when the weather was bad, winds blowing hard and snow piling up, and people depending on the Highway Department to keep things moving. It made him feel good that, because of him, someone sick could get to the hospital or someone alone could visit a friend or someone with a broken furnace could get help.

Harriet had to admit that she'd never looked at it that way and, yes, it was perhaps a noble calling if you thought about it. That pleased him. "A noble calling," he repeated. "You're very good with words, Harriet." If he were good with words, he told her, he would write about his work. He thought people would be amazed to know what it was like out there on the plow with the wind tossing bales of snow at you and the headlights of distant vehicles, like animal eyes, staring out of the whiteness at you.

When he returned Harriet to her booth and thanked her, Rose said of his retreating figure, "Ernie's stuck on you."

"Well, I'm not stuck on him. He's nice, but that's all."

"Sure wish he'd look *my* way," Rose complained.

"Why don't you ask him for ladies' choice?"

"I always think I'm going to, but I always chicken out. I'm not shy with the others. I could ask Cary Grant to dance. But at the last minute I never can get myself to ask Ernie."

"I never knew you were interested."

"At my age it embarrasses me to talk about a man that way when he shows no interest. Do you understand?"

Harriet did. It wasn't just embarrassment, though. It was superstition, too. If you talked too freely about your hopes, you seemed to invite disaster, to bring it down on yourself. After Bill Hahn had left for that good-paying job in Greenland, Harriet had all but quit talking aloud about romantic possibilities.

"Do you think it's silly for women our age to flirt and be . . . infatuated and, well, whatever?" Rose asked.

Harriet was tired of Rose talking about them as though they were old ladies with gnarled blue veins and smelly corsets. "We're *not* that old, Rose! We're still warm-blooded animals, if you understand my meaning. We keep ourselves up and we wear nice clothes. Any man should be proud to be seen with us. I don't feel the least silly."

Now and then she did shiver with doubt. Was it time to stop coming to the dances and join the Ladies' Aid Circle at the Methodist Church? But when that crossed her mind, the blood drained out of her face and hands and she felt stone dead for a minute.

"I was afraid you might take a shine to Ernie," Rose said, "since he's shown so much interest in you."

"He's not my type. He's very nice, but I'm not romantically inclined toward him."

"He talks beautifully, don't you think? Like poetry."

Yes, he did. He seemed intelligent and not at all common. Why *wasn't* she attracted to Ernie? Wouldn't it be lovely and simple if she were? He was someone Kate and Bess would like. He could be like a father to Bess. But you couldn't talk yourself into love any more than you could talk yourself out of it.

The next number was the "Beer Barrel Polka," and Billy and the Six Fat Goats played a particularly frenzied arrangement of it. DeVore, all angles and loping limbs, was headed toward her. Her heart beat so hard, she wished she could scream and release some of its fury.

Off they galloped, his wiry arms with their knotty,

workman's muscles holding her lightly, confidently. Harriet glimpsed Bess standing in the entrance. Bess and several others, Donna Olson among them, were crowded into the doorway surveying the dancers. One of the fellows, a soldier, detached himself and went to search for an empty booth.

Harriet was swept away to the opposite end of the floor, where she couldn't see Bess, and when she and DeVore whirled back around, Bess and the others had disappeared.

DeVore walked Harriet to her booth, something he didn't always do. Sometimes he left her at the edge of the dance floor, saying, "Well, I'll see you before long, I guess." Harriet was surprised and flustered when he sat down. Had he noticed her dancing with Ernie and been suddenly visited by the green-eyed monster? Or was he perhaps interested in Rose, who, at that moment, returned, flushed and laughing, from the dance floor? That could certainly be the case since Billy, the bandleader, announced the butterfly, and DeVore, turning to Rose, who looked quite pretty with her cheeks pink and her nose shiny, asked, "Are you ladies up to a butterfly?"

As they danced, DeVore holding first one and then the other of them, Harriet felt a knee-weakening fear. The floor seemed to fall away from under her. What if DeVore was really attracted to Rose and he'd struck up an acquaintance with her, Harriet, in order to meet her friend? Oh, wouldn't it be an awful irony if Ernie was stuck on *her* and DeVore was stuck on Rose?

Suddenly she saw Bess again—dancing the butterfly with Doyle Hanlon and Earl Ingbretson. Married men.

What on earth was she doing with them? Were their wives along? She caught Bess's eye and nodded. A nod was all she could manage, so great were her fears and jealousy over DeVore.

Later, Harriet saw the booth, or, rather, two booths where Bess and Donna were sitting. They were back where the light was dim, far from the dance floor, but at the kitchen end of the room so that Harriet could glimpse the girls now and again. My, didn't they look pretty in their pale summer cottons. Their bare arms were so firm, their faces so fresh. To be young and pretty and without care. It seemed almost unfair. Harriet chided herself. Envy was common, and it gave your face a hardened look.

Bess and Donna were in a party that included the soldier, another lad who looked to be his brother, Doyle Hanlon, and Earl Ingbretson. Bess was sitting with Doyle and Earl, Donna with the others. Harriet could not imagine how such a party came to be made up. That the girls should be with the soldier and his brother seemed reasonable enough. The two boys were young and looked not quite finished around the edges. But Doyle Hanlon must be twenty-five and Earl Ingbretson was closer to thirty. It was obviously an innocent arrangement, but it piqued Harriet's curiosity.

As Harriet watched, Doyle Hanlon got to his feet. He held his hand out to Bess and she took it. They walked toward the dance floor, his hand at Bess's back proprietarily. Now he was saying something clever and Bess, as they passed beneath a fly-specked yellow bulb, was gazing up at him with an expression on her face that Harriet had never seen there before.

"Oh dear me, no," Harriet whispered.

"Anything wrong?" Rose inquired.

"No. Nothing." Instantly the maternal and protective part of Harriet began poring over the slim data she possessed regarding Doyle Hanlon. Son of Rebecca and Herbert Hanlon. Husband of Jean Hanlon. Father of . . . well, a father, at any rate. Twenty-four years old? Twenty-five? Most likely twenty-five at least, since he'd been in college *and* Korea, though hadn't she heard that he'd shot himself in the foot to get out of Korea early? She didn't know whether to believe that. It was assumed in Harvester that if you had money, there was crookedness somewhere in your family and probably insanity as well. Only tainted blood could produce wealth.

Neither of the senior Hanlons was from these parts. St. Louis or New Orleans, Harriet thought. They both had a lingering tinge of accent. Rebecca Hanlon, who was only about five years older than Harriet, was as gracious and kind a woman as any in town, but not one to talk about herself. That was because of the way her husband had made his money when he'd come here during hard times, Harriet had decided. After all, the very clothes Rebecca Hanlon wore and the food she ate came to her through the tragedy of others. Little wonder she was always generous and ready to help.

Little wonder, too, that Herbert Hanlon was one who kept to himself. Not many men around in the thirties had been ready to pal with him. A few bankers, maybe. What kind of man had the stomach to pick other men's bones? Harriet shuddered. She had some knowledge of Herbert Hanlon's vulturing. Thank God DeVore's family hadn't lost their land to Hanlon.

But Harriet was a slave to fairness. Had she a family crest, Bess had once told her, the motto would read, "On the Other Hand . . ." She could not, therefore, dismiss from her mind the image of Herbert Hanlon carrying his wife in his arms—in and out of St. John's Episcopal Church, in and out of Rebecca's friends' homes—wherever Rebecca's interests took her. Hanlon himself did not attend these functions, but he did not deny his wife. He lifted her from her wheelchair as gladly and easily as if she were a child. And twining her arms around his neck, Rebecca cast her husband a very private glance, a look of gay intimacy that caught one unprepared and twisted one's heart with envy.

What sort of offspring did a couple like that produce? A coldhearted skirt chaser who pursued young girls? Or was Doyle Hanlon something else entirely? Whatever he was, he was not for Bess. The look Harriet had seen on Bess's face, she tried to put down to her own imagination. She was borrowing trouble. She was good at that. But a worry headache was tightening around her head, squeezing it like a lemon.

Massaging her temple, she turned her thoughts toward DeVore. That did not relieve the headache. Half an hour passed, during which he did not request a dance of her. When he wasn't schottisching with the divorcée from Ula, he was laughing with his sons. Several times Harriet thought he was looking toward her booth, but not at her, at Rose, or at the empty place where Rose would be if she weren't dancing. The bandleader announced ladies' choice, a set of slow waltzes.

"If you're interested in Ernie, go ask him to dance," Harriet told her friend. "Tonight's the night. If you don't ask him, I'll ask him for you."

"No, you don't."

"Then you do it."

"I'm scared."

"Of course you are, but you can be scared and still be brave. Get going or I'll tell him you wanted to but were too shy."

Rose pulled herself out of the booth but still hung back. Harriet started to get up.

"All right. All right. I'm going," Rose said, her voice shrill with nerves. "I wish I'd never told you about Ernie."

Untrue, thought Harriet, who was feeling staunch and maternal. She realized, however, that her own motives were questionable. Wasn't she pushing Rose at Ernie to keep her out of DeVore's way? On the other hand, she did honestly hope that Rose would find true and lasting happiness with Ernie.

She sipped warm beer. Sipping beer passed the time. It made you look occupied when no one asked you to dance. And she certainly wasn't going to ask DeVore for ladies' choice. What was the point of chasing after a man who was backing away? You'd end up falling on your face.

The dark-haired divorcée was leading DeVore to the

floor. Well, thought Harriet, she'll soon find out that he's quicksilver.

Or maybe she wouldn't. Maybe she'd be the one he chose for his wife. After all, she was broken in.

In the light of cruel but honest appraisal, Harriet saw that her dreams about DeVore had been built on nothing but desperate hope. She was deeply humiliated by her silliness and wished that she were not here in this grimy, sordid-looking place where you snagged your stockings on the booths and no one ever wiped off the tables, and the sound of empty laughter and shouted obscenities was deafening.

In DeVore's booth Lyle elbowed Delwin and pointed in Harriet's direction, laughing. Because she was staring straight ahead, they thought she couldn't see them, but her peripheral vision was excellent. They were laughing at her. What were they saying? "There's the old maid who's sweet on Pa. No way in hell he'd take up with her."

Rising slowly, she started toward the door, trying not to catch anyone's eye. The floor wobbled a little, and the walls, papered with lurid posters of coming attractions, tilted.

Outside, the midnight air was thick and hot as afternoon. No small breeze lifted the hair at her pinched temples. Beyond the parking lot, she sat down on dusty grass and hugged herself.

Twenty years ago, with fifteen dollars and a train ticket, Harriet had left Sioux City, left two old parents and two brothers who had always been indifferent toward her at best, and who had become resentful, even hostile, as she worked her way through business college while the boys became a shoe salesman and a hotel clerk, respectively. The family had resented her ambitions and her hoity-toity ways. Their lives weren't good enough for her. That was what they thought. And she'd been unable to convince them otherwise.

Kate and Martin had been different. They'd treated her with respect from the start, congratulating her cleverness when she landed a job with the Water and Power Company in the middle of hard times. The Drews had only recently lost their farm—well, *sold* it, but for pennies, and Harriet had been able to help out a little, paying them room and board. Harriet wasn't sure what would have happened to Kate and Martin if Kate's maiden aunt Hattie hadn't passed away, leaving a timely little legacy of several thousand to the Drews. Martin had been able to set up Drew's Body and Lube with his cousin Arnold and buy the house they'd been renting.

The Drews had been family to Harriet. Bess had been like a daughter to her. Even if Harriet didn't have DeVore Weiss, she still had Kate and Bess. And she had her career. Wasn't she office manager at the Water and Power Company, with half a dozen women working under her? Maybe this was her portion. It was a sight more than many women had. Why, then, was she craving all the time, craving something to wrap around her, as though she'd never in her life been warmed through?

At length she stood up, pulling her skirt around to check the back for dirt and grass. She was not going to vomit. She'd gotten past that. She'd better get back before

Rose had the police out looking for her. Rose. If Rose married Ernie and Harriet was left just to stand and watch, it would be time to join the Ladies' Aid Circle.

In the Dakota Ballroom, the madness had gone on without Harriet, the pounding beat of hundreds of feet bounding around the floor; below that, the heavy pulse of bass drum and tuba; above, the whine of accordion and the scream of cornet.

Through the big, open windows she saw the smear of dancers, like people caught on a wild carnival ride. Strains of a fast rendition of "Goodnight, Irene" blasted her like a hot wind from the Badlands.

There was DeVore in his blue plaid sports shirt, wheeling round and round with the short woman from Ula. And there, clinging to Ernie, was Rose in her red sheath that was too close-fitting across the abdomen and her short hair that was permed too tight. And wasn't that Bess with Doyle Hanlon, his right arm holding her waist close to him? How gracefully her back arched as she tossed her head, laughing at something he said.

Harriet wished that the night was over, and she and Bess were home with Kate.

CHAPTER 10

Bess

On the drive to the Dakota, Bess had sat in the front seat between Doyle and Earl, laughing as the two men razzed each other and teased her as well. That they might be vying with each other for her laughter hadn't occurred to her.

She didn't know much about men. Since Archer's death, she had had no men in her immediate family. Aunt Kate had told her to hang on to her memories of Uncle Martin so that she would always know what a good man was.

Because of their unfamiliarity, Bess was all the more drawn to men. Not that she imagined them to be more commendable than women, but their mystery was a challenge and attraction. For that reason she had heroes rather than heroines: Harry Truman, Laurence Olivier, Rupert Brooke, and Beethoven (never mind that those last two were long dead).

The appurtenances of masculinity intrigued and delighted her. They must be clues to what men were: the pleasant stench of beer and the smell of pipes and cigars (after ten years her great-uncle Martin's pipe smoke still lingered in Aunt Kate's house); the perfume of aftershave lotion and leather gloves; the bluish tinge on a jaw where whiskers had been shaved away; body hair and baldness; small mannerisms like the trouser-hitching-up that men were always performing when they stood up, even when their pants weren't falling down.

Great-uncle Martin had executed an elaborate hitching-up, but that had something to do with his hernia. Bess had never seen Uncle Martin or Archer or any man naked. She'd seen pictures of statues and paintings of naked men, but damned few. And mostly the sex organs in these were teensy, nothing to cause you to hitch your pants up all the time as if you were putting your unwieldy equipment away in some pocket inside your trousers. Maybe this trouser hoisting was merely a ritual, like backslapping and arm punching.

Bess studied the men on either side of her. Here was a glimpse into that masculine mystique about which she was ignorant. Here were two live specimens, and not just high school boys.

Of the two, Doyle Hanlon was the more handsome and also the more complicated and intriguing. Often Bess had dismissed boys who were exceptionally good-looking. Archer had possessed a beautiful face, and look what that had been worth. Handsome is as handsome does, Aunt Kate never tired of saying.

Then too, very good-looking boys frequently expected you to fall all over them. Doyle Hanlon wasn't like that. He was cocky, but it had nothing to do with his looks. His cockiness was full of self-mockery: hadn't he spoken of his limp as being distinguished? Did he really limp, she wondered, or did he only imagine that he did? Or was the limp a condition to which he'd become wedded and from which he could not be divorced, though it had ceased to exist? Or was it a ruse for attracting girls like Bess? No. It wasn't a ruse.

By the time Jim Arliss had found booths for them and they'd ordered beers, it was eleven. Two hours of music left. The Dakota was not a grand place. It was dimly lit, for very good reasons, and hazy with smoke, especially in winter when the windows were shut. The booths were sticky with ancient beer and sweat, and a woman was a fool to wear a good dress there, but women did anyway.

Bess and Boyd and Earl danced a butterfly. Donna and the Arlisses were in front of them. Across the way Harriet and Rose danced with DeVore Weiss. Bess felt a stab of anger. Would Harriet actually break up the family she'd been part of for years to marry that long-necked gander? He probably hadn't cracked a book since high school, if then. Bess was sure his kids were illiterates. Why would someone like Harriet want to mother a bunch of illiterates who smelled of sour milk and cow manure?

A long time ago, Harriet had put her arms around Bess and promised never to leave her. She'd sat on the back step holding Bess and telling her the wonderful things they would do together—flying on airplanes and seeing things that almost no one in Harvester had ever seen. In all their talks after Celia's death, hadn't it been implicit that Harriet would always belong to Bess? Who would ever love Harriet's pretensions and her scrawniness as Bess did?

Harriet nodded to Bess but didn't smile. Clearly she

was provoked to see Bess with a married man. Well, Bess was just as provoked with her and she wasn't going to smile either.

If Harriet married DeVore Weiss, then that was that. No way would Bess take her back. Bess did not feel good about this, but she felt certain.

The bandleader announced "The Tennessee Waltz" and Doyle asked Bess to dance. A plump woman in a vivid print jersey dress who was breaking in with Billy and the Six Fat Goats had begun to sing, trying hard to sound like Patti Page.

As Bess and Doyle made their way toward the floor, he joked, "If I see any old friends, don't expect me to introduce you." Bess laughed, flattered that this clever, handsome man would make such an allusion to the lyrics, but realizing at the same time that it wasn't quite proper. She wasn't his "true love," after all.

The entire evening with him was not quite proper. Not scandalous. They were in a group. They'd done nothing indecent. But it would be scandalous if it happened again. A cold current of loneliness brushed her brow. Spinning between the other couples, finding the paths of least resistance, they were dancing on an ice floe, cut off from custom.

"'I remember the night and the Tennessee Waltz . . .'" the vocalist belted, a mournful catch in her voice.

"What are you going to study at college?" Doyle asked as they danced.

"Literature, I think."

"What do you like to read?"

"Poetry. Novels. D. H. Lawrence when I can get hold of him. Waugh, Huxley, Fitzgerald, Faulkner."

"And what will you do with them? Teach?"

"I hope not."

"Why?"

"I don't like kids," she said, forgetting that Doyle Hanlon was a father. "I like grown-ups."

"How can you tell the difference?"

"What do you mean?"

"Take me, for example. Do I look grown up?"

"Yes."

"Well, I'm not. I'm a spoiled kid. I ran away to the army to grow up and got a busted leg instead."

Was he trying to warn her, or was he simply making self-deprecating conversation? If he were warning her, wasn't that presumptuous? Did he assume that she was becoming infatuated with him? Bess wished that she could see her face in a mirror and know what showed there. Did she look confused and light-headed, warm one minute and cold the next?

Jim Arliss asked her for the next dance.

"When do you have to go back?" she asked.

"Monday."

"That's not much time."

"I wish to hell I wasn't going back."

"I can imagine." Her words sounded insincere in her ears. She was glad he was leaving because he seemed the kind of boy who could be persistent and troublesome. Yet she did feel sorry for him. She wished him away, but not to war.

"I'm not yellow," he assured her.

"I didn't think you were."

"I'm point man in my platoon."

"What's that?"

"The point man goes first. If there's a mine in the road or snipers, he catches it."

"My God."

"I'm not trying to make out that I'm a hero. Somebody has to be point man. I've never even skinned a knee over there, so they call me 'Lucky.' With a name like that, I figure I have to be the point man."

Jim wasn't drunk, but he'd had quite a few beers and maybe he had a bottle tucked away somewhere and was ordering setups. In any case, he was speaking more slowly and precisely than earlier.

"You with that guy?" he asked.

"What guy?"

"You know what guy. The one that was in Korea. The one that drove you out here."

"Well, he's not my date, if that's what you mean. He just gave me a ride, like you and Bob gave Donna a ride."

"You could come with us."

He was right. There was plenty of room in their car, but she hadn't wanted to go with them.

"You letting him take you home?" he asked.

"I'll get a ride with him," Bess explained, resenting the question but not daring to ignore the implications. She didn't want it noised all over St. Bridget County that she was seeing a married man. "But so will Earl," she told Jim. "I'll be dropped off before Earl, if that answers your question."

He looked unconvinced. "If you're worried about your reputation, let me and Bob take you home."

Again, Bess didn't answer. She was angry. What right had this Jim Arliss?

"I can show you a good time," he continued. "You learn a lot over there, and it ain't all about killing gooks."

"I'm not looking for a 'good time,'" Bess told him. "What do you think I am?" So much for decent Catholic boys. But he probably was a decent Catholic boy who'd learned too many things in the war and had had too much to drink tonight.

"What do I think you are? I think you're somebody making eyes at a married man. And he's making them back at you."

"And I think you're drunk."

"Sorry," he said, oddly contrite.

At the end of the song, he saw her back to her booth. "I'm going to ask you again," he said. He still wanted to take her home.

Bess felt trapped, and it was her own doing. She didn't want Jim Arliss to take her home. She wasn't attracted to him, and he'd expect her to neck with him in the backseat of the car all the way to Harvester. He'd end up angry at the perfunctory good-night kiss, which was all he could expect, and it would have been a handshake if he weren't headed back to Korea.

Plenty of boys had gotten only a handshake after seeing her home from a dance. More than one had complained to his buddies that she was a frigid, stuck-up bitch. If the boy was returning her home from an event for which he'd called and asked her out, she kissed him good night. It seemed only fair. Occasionally she found a boy with whom she really wanted to neck, but those had been few and far between.

She wondered why it was that the boys she liked—the ones with sufficient brains and character—were generally the ones without sex appeal. She realized that when it came to sex appeal, there were no absolutes. One girl's heartthrob was another girl's deadly bore. But in the unique world of her own tastes, the sexy boys rarely carried on an intelligent conversation, and after a couple of evenings of necking with them, Bess lost interest; whereas, try as she might, she could seldom get herself heated up over the boys with whom she enjoyed talking. Why wasn't she one of the lucky girls who enjoyed necking with everybody?

"He wants to take you home," Doyle observed of Jim Arliss. "It's all right if you want to go."

"I don't."

"Then don't." As he spoke, he grasped between his thumb and forefinger the fabric of Bess's sleeve, which had become crushed, and perked it up to its former fullness. It was an oddly intimate act, not lost on Bess.

"I feel guilty."

"About not going with him?"

She nodded.

"It's the uniform."

"Is it?"

When the next ladies' choice, a set of three slow waltzes, was announced, Bess asked Doyle. She could see that Jim Arliss was disappointed and angry, but maybe now he would give up the idea of taking her home. If he told everyone in the country that she was seeing Doyle Hanlon, what could she do?

But she worried about Aunt Kate. Kate had had enough scandals. If word got back to her that her grandniece was seeing Doyle Hanlon, Bess didn't know what it would do to her. Of course, she wasn't seeing him, only letting him give her a ride home. But people misinterpreted innocent acts, especially if you'd had a drunken father. If you had a riffraff father like Archer, they believed anything of you.

"What happened to your smile?" Doyle asked during the waltzes. "You're not letting the soldier spoil your evening, are you?" He squeezed her hand as if to waken her.

CHAPTER 11

Kate

Leaving the stove light burning in the kitchen and flicking on the porch light, Kate set out for Frieda's. More and more, even these few steps across the street were a painful adventure. Frieda always said, "Arnold will come with the car." But Kate didn't want Arnold to come with the car. You had to keep going on your own steam as long as you could.

Kate did not like to think about becoming a cripple. Dr. White had said, "There's not much that we can do about this kind of arthritis, Kate. Try to keep moving."

"How long before I can't move?"

He had shrugged. "Couldn't say. The disease can slow down, even stop its progress. I've heard of that."

Maybe. *If* she forgave Archer. But if the crippling didn't slow down, what then? She would *not* allow Bess to care for her. She would not allow the child to be tied down that way.

And her herbs—chamomile oil and comfrey poultices and such—hadn't relieved the stiffening. But how could they, since hate was what caused it?

If she were unable to get around, she would have to give

up the house. That thought made her dizzy with panic. She stopped and looked back at the place where she'd lived since they had lost the farm and moved to town.

This was the house where she'd learned to live in town, as well as she ever *had* learned. What she had endured here over these twenty-some years and what she had loved here were impressed upon the wallpaper and into the grain of the oak floors. To leave the house would be to leave witness and friend.

What would become of her? Would she live at the Friendship Arms Nursing Home at the west end of town? She smiled at the small, sour joke in her mind. *Going west.* To die. Well, she hoped that was all a good distance down the line.

The move to town had crushed her to the point where she thought she would never recover. In some ways she never had. The farm was with her, waking and sleeping. And these past months, with her conjuring, it had been her sole refuge from pain. Still, this house had understood, had not taken offense.

She did not blame Martin for the loss of the farm. Hard times had taken it. Hard times had come early to farmers, long before the stock market crash. She and Martin had hung on way past the point when others might have given up. If it hadn't been for her garden, they would never have lasted as long as they did. You couldn't eat fields of feed corn and rye, and what those brought at market didn't pay for the seed. Thank God, the old folks had died before the farm was sold. They had died believing that Martin and Kate could hang on.

Fishing the soft linen handkerchief from the bodice of her dress, Kate dabbed at her eyes, provoked with herself for falling again into a bleak reverie. She was getting soft in the head.

Frieda was too adept at reading her mind. She would fuss if she thought that Kate was down in the dumps. Kate couldn't stand Frieda's fussing, so she'd better slap a smile on her face. Stepping down off the curb cautiously with one foot and then the other, Kate looked both ways and proceeded.

"You ought to find a husband," Frieda had been telling her since 1942. Martin had died in December of forty-one, and Frieda had allowed him eleven months in his grave before she had started in about finding a husband.

Ten years ago Frieda had said, "You're a young woman, only forty-nine. You should find a husband." Now she said, "You're a young woman, only fifty-nine. You should find a husband." Kate had never given a thought to finding another husband. For thirty years Martin had suited her entirely. She was all married out.

Besides, she enjoyed her life with Bess and Harriet. Hadn't these been good years, the three of them living together like three peas in a snug pod? This summer was the twilight of that, she supposed.

"Now, wouldn't it be nice if you had a husband?" Frieda asked, placing a dish of butter mints and peanuts in front of Kate. "Then we'd be a foursome for cards, you and me and Arnold and your mister. We wouldn't always have to depend on Marie Wall."

"My, the butter mints taste fresh. Did you buy them here in town?"

"Nah. We got them in St. Bridget."

"Anderson's should carry butter mints or Mather's or the drugstore. The mints at Truska's taste like they've been around since before the war."

"The Civil War." Frieda laughed and went to fetch the tally pad. Returning, she asked, "Where was Bess off to?"

"I don't know. She was meeting Donna Olson. They might go to the band concert, she said."

"It wouldn't hurt her to stay home once in a while and keep you company."

"But then you might not ask me for cards."

"She'll be gone soon. She should spend some time with you now."

"She's seventeen. Seventeen doesn't think that way. Did you when you were that age? Anyway, she's a good girl. She works hard and she should get out and have fun."

Frieda was childless, and her opinions about what children should or should not do reflected this. "Where would she be without you?" she asked. "It's for sure Archer didn't leave her anything." Frieda stood beside the bridge table, picking a butter mint from among the peanuts in the candy dish. She glanced sideways at Kate. "Speaking of Archer, Mabel Pickard was tongue-wagging about him at Study Club the other afternoon."

"In front of you?"

"Nah. I was in the kitchen. She didn't think I could hear."

"What was she on about?"

"Archer and the Jessup girl."

Dismayed, Kate shook her head. "Why now?"

"Some high school girl was sent to Chicago to 'look after her sick aunt' this spring, so of course the conversation got around to Archer."

Things always came back around to Archer.

"Remember the first time we saw him, I was with you?" Frieda asked, sitting down at the table and fussing with the tally pad and pencil, trying to fit the pencil, which was too large, into the loop provided for it on the pad.

Frieda had brought up the subject of Archer at least once a month for ten years. Of course Kate remembered. How would she forget?

"He was a good-looker," Frieda said. "Everyone on Main Street was gawking, trying to figure out who he was." She folded her hands together on the bridge table, fingers intertwined. "Such a clean white shirt he was wearing. Mrs. Jessup or the Jessup girl must have washed and ironed it for him."

It had been a hot night, like tonight, only it was Saturday, and Saturday nights everyone came to town and parked on Main Street. In those days the stores stayed open on Saturday nights so the farmers could do their shopping. Nowadays they didn't stay open *any* night.

Kate had looked forward to Saturday nights then in a way that she looked forward to nothing now. Archer had come in thirty-two. That year people didn't have much to look forward to, but still everyone looked forward to Saturday night.

Even if you didn't have a dime, you could stand on Main Street and jaw, or sit in your car, if you had one, and watch people parade by. And you'd holler to them if they didn't see you sitting there; "Nellie, Ivan, here! Here in the car." And they'd come over and say hello, put a foot up on the running board, lean on the door and see who was with you, tell you what was happening, how the grain was doing and how it would soon be time for threshing.

Anderson's Candy and Ice Cream, beside the Majestic Theater, did a land-office business. And Grandpa Hapgood set up his popcorn wagon down on the corner. Martin always bought the largest-size bag because he knew how Kate enjoyed it. They sat in the car and ate popcorn and talked to their friends.

That car was an old 1911 Model T Ford touring car that had come to Martin from his uncle Ernest, who'd been killed in an Oklahoma oil field accident. The Ford had seen better days when Martin came into it, but, bless his heart, he'd kept it running until 1935.

And Celia, when she was little, sat like a princess in the backseat as if the car were still as grand as it had once been. Or she settled on the curb beside the car with the pennies Martin gave her on Saturday nights. With quiet pride and patience she sat arranging them in patterns on the ground, putting them in her pocket, taking them out to play again, saving them until it was time to go home. When the stores were closing and the cars began to load up and leave, Martin would say, "I think it's time we got home, girls," and Celia would dash for Anderson's to buy candy to take home.

As she grew older, Celia met her girlfriends and they promenaded up and down Main Street, looking in Lundeen's windows, dropping into Mather's Five and Dime for bobby pins and ribbons, or into Haroldson's Pharmaceuticals.

The night they first saw Archer, Celia and her chums were sitting on the front fenders of the car giggling and talking about boys. Frieda was in the backseat and Kate was in the front. Martin had walked down to the pool hall to buy cigars.

Frieda had asked, "Now, who is *that*?"

Kate had been sitting sideways in the seat, and she turned to look where Frieda pointed. Coming up the street was a young fellow, maybe twenty-two or -three, dressed in dark trousers and a clean white shirt open at the neck. He had his hands in his pockets and he was whistling. He paused to scan the window of Mather's Five and Dime, and Kate wondered if he wasn't doing it to give Celia and the other girls time to notice him.

"Not from Harvester," Frieda had remarked. "A farmhand, I expect."

After a few minutes of looking over everything in the window, the young man had opened the screen door and gone in. A minute or so later he came out without any bag or box, his hands back in his pockets. Had he gone into Mather's to see how long he could hold the attention of the giggling girls sitting on the Drew car? As he had no doubt figured, they were waiting for him to reappear, though they pretended not to notice when he let the screen door to and continued down the street. As he passed, he nodded. "Ladies."

They studied his back as he strolled, without a seeming care, down Main Street, stopping at the popcorn wagon.

He paid for the popcorn, picked up the bag, and lifted it to his mouth without ever removing his left hand from his trousers. Somehow Kate knew there was something wrong with that hand.

At the corner he turned right, out of sight. Those girls would have given a good deal to have followed and seen what car he got into.

He had been a looker, all right, with straight dark hair that fell over one eye, skin tanned darker than an Indian's, and eyes a pale, shocking blue. His cheeks were high and prominent, and his eyes were long, and they tilted where the cheekbones rose. His jaw was hard and angular, his mouth almost without curve.

The face was full of something older than anger, some combination of resentment and deprivation. The girls on the street, and Frieda too, had been repelled at the same time that they were attracted. A year later Celia married him.

A knock came at Frieda's porch door and Kate was recalled from the past by Marie Wall's airy, girlish voice calling, "OK if I come in?"

Frieda's husband, Arnold, appeared from the kitchen, where he'd put the chocolate ice cream away in the freezing compartment. He hailed Marie as she tripped into the living room: "You going to help me take these two old ladies to the cleaner's, Marie?"

"Old ladies, are we?" Frieda snorted, shuffling the cards. "You hear that, Kate? These two old ladies'll teach you how to play cards, old man." Setting the deck down in front of

Marie Wall so that she could cut the cards, Frieda said, "Behave yourself, old man, and maybe Kate'll read your fortune later."

Arnold laughed. "My fortune's in the new grease rack," he said, referring to the latest wrinkle at Drew's Body and Lube.

"Oh, read mine, Kate," Marie implored, giving the deck a knock with her knuckles.

They played until midnight, when Constable Wall drove by on his way home. Then Frieda rang him to come for ice cream. And after Kate had read Marie's fortune, which she dressed up a bit since the unvarnished version was as exciting as boiled cabbage, the party broke up.

"Arnold'll drive you home," Frieda told Kate.

"No, he won't. I want to walk. If I stop walking, I'm done for."

Bess's handbag wasn't lying on the dining room table, where she usually tossed it. Nor was Harriet's Ford parked in the back driveway, so Kate left the stove light burning for them when she went up to bed. Dragging unwilling legs up each step was a test of her stubbornness. One of these days the stairs would be too much and she would have to put a bed in the sewing room, off the dining room. Not yet.

Old age was a forced retreat. You carried with you as much of what you had been as you could. Some of it—often the best of it—you had to abandon. Kate had had to give up the garden.

Wearing her nightgown of soft, much-washed white

muslin, she sighed, sitting down on the side of the bed. The walk to Frieda's and back had cost her. Easing her legs up onto the cool sheets, she closed her eyes and conjured herself back on the farm. She saw the jar of cosmos she had picked from the garden and set on the washstand beside the bed. She saw herself in the old rocking chair by the bedroom window, gazing down at the big garden, then turning to write in the journal book. However haphazardly, she tried to put something down in it two or three times a week.

The journal book is just an old ledger that Martin's mother has given her and into which she crams a miscellany of recipes, many for herbal remedies, along with thoughts and plans and letters from her sister Clara written after Clara married Chauncey in 1914. There are notes from Martin as well, two- or three-lined missives which he has tucked into her apron pocket over the years.

"To My Lady Farmer—I guess I tempted you into marrying me by holding out the farm as bait. But whether it was me or the farm that brought you here, it doesn't matter. I see that you love me almost as much as you love the place and that is all I need.

"From Your Country Man"

She is ever chastened by those words and regrets that Martin saw so well how things were. However, he was not chiding her for loving the farm so dearly, but reassuring her. And his generous nature has deepened her love for him.

In his notes Martin expresses what he cannot comfortably say aloud. When Clara and Chauncey were both struck down with influenza in 1917, he wrote: "If they God forbid die, we'll take Celia and love her more than sunshine."

And they took three-year-old Celia and loved her more than sunshine. She wasn't with them a week before they forgot that she hadn't always been there. Kate mourned her Clara. But Celia seemed to have grown out of Kate's heart.

Rising from the rocking chair, Kate lays the ledger on the washstand and climbs into bed, plumping the down pillow and arranging tired limbs. Martin has taken a lantern to the barn to check on a sick heifer.

Crying out, Kate lurched up in bed. Moving as quickly as she was able, she pulled back the single sheet that covered her and let her feet over the side of the bed. She'd heard a crash.

Where was Bess? Kate's cane stood against the bedside table. Reaching for it, she pushed herself up and shuffled to the window.

She brushed aside the lace curtain, looking down toward the corner of Second Street and Third Avenue. She was awake now and knew she would see no cars there, certainly no crumpled, mangled cars with torn bodies in them.

The dream recurred every few months. Each time she cried out and woke and shuffled to the window, even as she realized that it had been a dream. What if there were an accident down there? What if . . .

The Big Ben clock, whose alarm she never set, said one-thirty. She hobbled into the hall, not turning on a lamp. At Bess's door she looked in. Light from the street revealed an unmade bed covered with clothes and books but no girl. At Harriet's door it was the same, except that the bed was perfectly made and had no clothes lying on it, only a ruffled satin pillow Harriet had run up on her Singer.

In the bathroom Kate swallowed three aspirin with water. The headache was like an iron cap, and the dream had made it worse. She studied the face in the mirror above the sink. Her hair had gone white when Celia was killed, but her brows were still jet.

Making her way back to bed, Kate left the sheet off. She was perspiring. The room was breathless. She stared at the ceiling's white-on-white-patterned wallpaper. She didn't want to fall asleep until she knew that Bess was safe.

These panics came over her now and again and she couldn't reason with them. If only she knew where Bess was. Was she in someone's car? Maybe she'd run across Harriet and Rose and joined up with them. But Bess and Harriet rarely came home together. Each had her own friends, her own haunts.

Kate clenched her hands into fists and searched the wallpaper for hidden signs, bleached entrails, snowy foretokens of an untroubled dawn.

CHAPTER 12

Bess

Bess was with Doyle Hanlon. Ten minutes before the strains of "Goodnight, Sweetheart" were struck up, and while Jim Arliss was dancing with Donna, Bess and Doyle and Earl Ingbretson walked out of the Dakota and piled into Doyle's car.

Bess had taken Donna aside and told her that she, too, was welcome to ride home in Doyle Hanlon's car. But Donna said no. She'd danced most of the past two hours with Bob Arliss, who was a nice boy and sober, so she would let him take her home.

"I'll stop in the Loon tomorrow and let you know how it went," she said, examining her lipstick in a mirror no bigger than her thumb.

So, at a quarter to one, Bess squeezed into the car again between the two men. They'd all been up since early morning and would have to be up in the next day's early morning, so conversation was less antic than during the drive over.

Doyle and Earl discussed a ten-day fishing trip that Earl and his family were taking to Leech Lake. His wife, Barbara, wasn't worth a tinker's dam with a rod and reel,

Earl said, but he was damned if he was going to do without a fishing trip this year. Barbara had known he liked to fish when she married him.

"Why don't you go alone?" Bess ventured.

"What kind of vacation would that be for her?"

"You're a son of a bitch," Doyle said without rancor.

Although seated benignly, hands folded, Bess was thrashing around in her mind, panicked, ecstatic, and depressed. She felt compelled to jump out of the car and run across the fields, to save herself. Simultaneously she wanted never to get out of the car at all, but to cling to the steering wheel or door handle until someone dragged her bodily from it. An aching had taken hold of her. She was a little delirious, she thought.

Doyle braked for the stop sign where the road met County Road 14, then swung right, heading toward Harvester. No stop sign had stood at this crossing the night that Archer missed the turning, if "missed" was the right word. Resting her head against the back of the seat, Bess closed her eyes, shutting out the cottonwood grove and the Jessup farm.

They drove slowly into Harvester, now mostly closed down. "Anyone want to stop at the all-night?" Doyle asked.

"I gotta get home," Earl said. "The old lady's gonna have a fit." But his house was dark when they stopped to let him out. Barbara hadn't waited up.

Earl opened the car door. "Behave," he said. Was that something he always said, or was it meant for Doyle? Did Doyle often misbehave?

Doyle Hanlon turned right at Eighth Street, in the direction of Bess's house. "You know where I live?" she asked. Why was it hard to speak?

He nodded, and they drove in silence. At Eighth and Third Avenue, he said, "Could we ride around for half an hour?"

"It's pretty late."

"Don't be afraid. I just want to be with you. You can say 'Take me home' anytime, and I will."

Bess said nothing. Doyle Hanlon had power over her. This must be what people meant by "chemistry" between a man and a woman. Chemistry had her in its grip.

Slowly, because they were not going anywhere, they rode up and down country lanes, windows wide open, while the radio played softly, a powerful station from far away—Chicago or somewhere. A clear-channel station.

On the gravel roads, the Mercury's headlights picked out jackrabbits and raccoons, and in the tall, dusty grass, they caught little burning eyes staring out. Across air heavy with clover and black earth, fields of corn whispered.

Drifting as far north as Ula, Doyle swung the car back toward Harvester. If he had driven to the far side of the earth, Bess would not have had the starch to say "Take me home."

He reached for her hand and she gave it to him, her heart swooping and curveting wildly in the sky.

Five miles from town, he pulled the car to the side of the road, stopping beneath a row of box elders, part of an old grove. Yes, she had expected this.

With the engine off, the sound of crickets was deafening. In the distance a farm dog barked, and close at hand a rotted fence post creaked. Doyle took her hand again.

"I want to kiss you good night," he said. "And I won't be able to do that in town."

Would he think that she let just anyone kiss her? She wanted to explain that she didn't, but she could think of no way to put it that wasn't trite, so she said nothing. For the first time she did not critically analyze a kiss as it was happening but let its warm syrup pour through her and, when it ended, felt a keen privation.

"I want to see you again," he told her. "Will you meet me at the Lucky Club tomorrow night? Tonight," he amended, glancing at the dashboard clock.

She didn't answer. He looked at her so solemnly that she turned away from him, feeling weighed down by his gaze. After a moment, he started the engine and they continued back to town.

Stopping at the corner of Second Street, several houses from Kate's, he cut the lights but not the engine. When he looked at Bess, she smiled and touched his hand, which lay on the steering wheel. He smiled gravely back.

"You don't have to decide now," he said. "I'll call you tomorrow."

"I'll be working."

"At the Loon?"

"Seven-thirty to three-thirty."

"I'll come in for coffee. Is that all right?"

"Of course."

She hurried across the intersection and up Second Street

to Kate's house, watching Doyle Hanlon's taillights disappear. Trembling, she ran up the steps and inside, letting the screen door quietly close behind her. She mustn't wake Aunt Kate, who would ask what she had been doing.

Closing the door of her room with care so that a tiny click was the only sound, Bess threw the rumpled clothes from the bed onto a chair. Without turning on the light, she undressed, tossing her things onto the same chair and climbing into bed without a gown. She kicked the sheet and spread to the bottom of the bed and lay exposed to the darkness. Pretending that her hands were Doyle Hanlon's, she ran them over her face and breasts and down her belly.

Celia, is this what happened to you?

CHAPTER 13

Kate

ARCHER STOOD, as he often did, at the foot of Kate's bed, a darker stain within the darkness of the room. She left off talking with him when she heard a car stopping at the corner and then the screen door twanging downstairs.

Bess was home, although later than usual. The Big Ben alarm said two-fifteen.

Up the stairs the child came, quietly, stepping (Kate knew) to the side of the tread, close to the wall, to keep the stairs from creaking. She didn't stop in the bathroom to wash her face, but went straight along to her room and closed the door.

Archer waited.

How would Bess get into that bed with all the clothes and books piled on it? Kate massaged the swollen knuckles of her right hand. After a minute of listening to soft to-ing and fro-ing in the next room, she heard Bess's bedsprings gave a metallic wheeze and the house was still.

Kate sighed. In the account book of her mind, she ticked off another night, only a handful remaining until Bess would be away. *Elizabeth Canby escaped without injury.*

Her eyes again sought the dark figure at the foot of her bed.

"If I'd had it out with you, Archer, the night that Celia came running here with Bess . . .

"I know you hit her because there were marks on her cheek, but there was more to it, something awful, because she stayed with me a week." Fretful, Kate scraped her fingers back and forth across her brow.

"I guess I still had a speck of pity for you," she went on. "The war was off and running, and everybody was going except the older men and 4-Fs. You wanted to play soldier and you got half-crazy with loathing that useless arm.

"You'd've got killed doing some dramatic thing, I don't doubt. You yearned for a reckless end, like the end of a gangster movie.

"You were so miserable, they had to let you go at the lumberyard. They couldn't have someone dealing with the public who snarled like a cur. I think they were about to give you the boot at the creamery, too. But you showed them. You showed us all."

A little mewl of frustration hummed in her throat.

"If I'd gone to you the night that Celia came running here . . . but Martin was only dead eight months, and I kept thinking that having it out with you was something a *man* should do."

Disgust at her long-ago failure hardened her voice. "But a woman must do things." Like Demeter braving Hades to bring back Persephone.

Impatiently she dismissed Archer and turned her gaze once more to the white-on-white pattern of the ceiling. In the intricate web of silvery leaves lay intimations of things that a woman must do.

CHAPTER 14

Harriet

HARRIET WOKE AT SIX, not a bit tired, though it was only three hours since she had slipped out of her heels on the front stoop, crept in the door, and flicked off the porch light.

The morning was brilliantly sunny. The birds were pandemonious, as Kate liked to say, kicking up such a racket that a person couldn't sleep, even if she weren't half-dying to be up, announcing good news.

Harriet swung her legs over the bed and wiggled her feet into feathery mules. She would have to buy a pair of practical slippers now and save her feathery mules for special. Pulling on a light cotton robe, she made the bed and bustled along to the bathroom, humming Rodgers and Hammerstein as she went.

Descending the stairs, the mules clunked and Harriet was afraid she'd wake up Kate. She didn't ordinarily wear mules coming downstairs, except on weekends. Well, Kate had probably gone to bed early and wouldn't mind the noise.

Harriet wasn't going to the Water and Power Company this morning. She was taking a half day off. She would call in later and tell them she had a doctor's appointment. No, she'd better say a dentist's appointment because she didn't want them thinking she was pregnant, which they probably would when they heard she was getting married.

Suddenly she felt faint. Married. Hanging on to the stove, she made for the stool, crying like a fool. She groped in her pocket for a hanky. When she'd used up the hanky, she grabbed the hand towel from the rack beside the sink. Finally she found the box of Kleenex that Kate kept on the windowsill beside the African violets. Dabbing and blowing, she mopped up the ravages of her new happiness, then patted cold water from the open tap onto her puffy red face. She glanced up to see Kate at the door.

"What on earth is the matter?" Kate asked.

"Nothing. Nothing is the matter." Harriet's laugh came out squawky and high-pitched, like an exotic birdcall. She could see that Kate thought she was hysterical.

"Well, what is it then?" Kate started across the kitchen, looking as though she might give Harriet a shake to settle her down.

Harriet swung about, throwing her long arms around Kate in so ruthless a manner that the other woman winced. "I'm getting married!" Then, grabbing Kate's hands, Harriet tippy-toe danced before her like a child needing to be led to the bathroom.

Freeing a hand, Kate groped for the stool. "Married," she breathed. "Married." Lowering herself carefully onto the seat, she blinked several times and put a hand to her head as though she'd bumped it on a cabinet door.

"Aren't you happy?" Harriet yelled, feeling in herself such a source of power and energy as she had never known.

A brand-new engine was running her and she could not stand still.

Grabbing the coffeepot, she filled it with water and coffee, then plugged it in with a flourish. From the bread box she pulled a loaf of raisin bread and dropped two slices into the toaster.

"Eggs?" she asked Kate, sliding the iron skillet out of the oven.

"What?"

"Would you like eggs, darling Kate?"

"No . . . no. Not this morning."

"I think I will," Harriet twittered, throwing open the refrigerator door as if it were the gateway to the future. "I'm hungry enough to eat a cow." She withdrew eggs, butter, homemade peach jam, and a bottle of orange juice. "I didn't get in until three. But I woke up at six like I'd been shot out of a gun."

Carrying the jam, plates, and silverware into the dining room, Harriet began laying the breakfast table, never missing a beat in her narrative. "You're probably wondering how all this came about. I'm sort of knocked off my pins, myself. I'm pinching myself black and blue, Kate."

Pulling two juice glasses from the cupboard, Harriet filled them and returned the bottle to the refrigerator.

"That bottle's empty, Harriet," Kate pointed out.

"What?" Harriet glanced at the empty orange juice bottle and doubled over laughing. "I was going to put an empty bottle in the refrigerator!"

"Yes."

When Harriet finally reined in her laughter, she put

the bottle in the sink and began to fry three eggs. Never in her life had she eaten three eggs at breakfast; never in her life had she been engaged.

"Well—to begin—Rose and I went to the Old Time dance, as planned."

Kate nodded.

"Everything was sort of the same as it always is at the Old Time. Kate, would you push the toaster down?" Harriet recalled seeing Bess at the Dakota Ballroom in the company of a married man, but she would say nothing of that. "I danced with DeVore Weiss and some others, and so did Rose." She turned the eggs gently, then carried the skillet to the dining room and slid them onto her plate. Returning the pan to the kitchen, she buttered the toast.

Kate shuffled into the dining room in her moccasin slippers. Ahead of her Harriet swooped and glided and trilled like one of the early morning birds.

"Late in the evening, Kate, I got this awful feeling that I was making a fool of myself—thinking that DeVore Weiss was interested in me. All of a sudden it seemed to me that it was Rose he was stuck on and that he'd sort of used me to get to know her. Can you imagine how depressed I was?" She reached across the table to grab hold of Kate's hand, but Kate's hands were folded in her lap, so Harriet absently brushed invisible crumbs into a pile beside the jam jar.

"I was so depressed, I went outside and sat on the grass under a tree. I sat there a long time. Rose said I was missing for so long, she thought I'd gotten sick and gone to the car, but I was just sitting feeling embarrassed and sorry for myself.

"It was time for the last dance when I went back in. All the men were rushing around looking for the one they wanted to take home. And here comes DeVore saying, 'Where in hell've you been? I was about to send the cops out lookin'.'

"I couldn't believe my ears. He'd never said anything of a romantic nature like that. I was dancing about six inches off the ground. Then, while we were waltzing, he asked me, 'You got a way home?' Well, of course I did, since I'd come in Rose's car, but I didn't want to say that for fear that'd be the end of it, so I said, 'I don't know.' Can you believe it? I lied on my feet as if I'd been doing it all my life."

The narrative was interrupted for a bite of egg. "Wouldn't you know it, last night this fellow named Ernie asked Rose home, so today I've got to drive her over to Red Berry to pick up her car at the Dakota. Well, that's a small price to pay, wouldn't you say?

"When we left the dance, I thought DeVore would bring me right home. He has to get up with the roosters. I didn't care, I was so happy to be going with him. But instead he stops at the all-night and orders their best steak, one for him and one for me.

"He said to the Arnoldsen boy, 'Give us a pair of your best steaks. One for me and one for the lady,' just as much as announcing to the world that I was his girlfriend."

Harriet rose and went to the kitchen for the coffeepot,

cups, and saucers. Returning, she poured two cups, pushing one across the table to Kate. "You haven't drunk your juice or eaten your toast."

Resuming her seat, she continued as though there had been no pause in the story. "While we were eating, half the county came in there, gawking like we were prize hogs at the county fair. A couple of them were farmer friends of DeVore's, and they came over to the booth to say hello and look me over.

"DeVore didn't pay them much mind, but just chatted casually, like it was the most normal thing in the world for him to be sitting with me.

"When we finished the steaks, we ordered ice cream. And DeVore said, 'I thought maybe you'd got a better offer.'

"'What do you mean?' I asked him.

"'When you were gone so long from the dance, I thought maybe you'd gone for a walk with another guy.'

"'I was feeling a little light-headed from the heat, was all, so I went out to get some fresh air,' I told him.

"'I'm glad that's all it was,' he said, and I nearly keeled over in my strawberry ice cream.

"It was almost half past two when we left the all-night. 'You're going to be a zombie in the morning,' I told DeVore, 'staying out all night like this.'

"'Don't you worry,' he said. 'When I'm feeling good, I can go without sleep a couple of days.' He was like that from the time he asked me for the last dance, saying one sweet thing after another. He's quite the romantic swain when he gets going.

"He knew right where I lived. I don't think I ever told

him that, but he drove right up to the house, like he'd been doing it for years. I started to get out and he said, 'What's your big hurry? Will Missus Drew turn on the porch light?' He's got a wonderful sense of humor. You're going to laugh when you know him.

"Would you think I could be this hungry when I ate like a thresher four hours ago?" After a few more bites of the toast and egg, washed down with coffee, she laid down her fork. She was staring at the coffee cup, and as she spoke she kept her eyes glued to it.

"He started to kiss me, and I said, 'I don't think we should do this the very first time you bring me home. I don't want you thinking I'm fast.'

"Then he said, 'What if we were engaged? Would it be all right then?'

"I asked him what that meant because I thought it was some kind of joke and I didn't like it.

"'I mean, if I ask you to marry me, will you let me kiss you?'

"'If you ask me to marry you and you *mean* it and aren't just playing with me, you can kiss me till the cows come home,' I told him.

"Then he started kissing me and he was getting pretty serious and I still wasn't sure we understood each other, so I pulled away and asked him, 'Is it all right if I announce the engagement in the paper?'

"'Hell, you can put it on the radio if you want,' he said.

"We kissed for about ten minutes, and then I told him he had to go home because I was too excited about the engagement to go on kissing.

"'I don't think the cows have come home yet,' he said, and he gave me a couple more kisses just to show who was boss.

"He's coming to the house tonight to meet you, so you can see how serious it is."

She daintily applied peach jam to one of the small bits of toast, took a generous bite, and wiped her mouth with a napkin. "I'm so happy, words fail me, as they say."

Kate said nothing.

CHAPTER 15

Kate

After Harriet went upstairs to take a bath, Kate hobbled to the daybed on the porch. She could not afford to think about Harriet's marriage. Not yet. She wasn't ready to face the loss it would mean, the changes it would bring.

Her fingers plucked abstractedly at the ripple-weave spread while memory, like the strong retreating tide that carries the struggling bather out to sea, carried her where she did not wish to go.

On that horrid afternoon in 1930, she'd thought, Dear God, don't let life change. Don't let it change the way that Martin is saying it must.

"We can't hang on," he'd told her. "They're taking the tractor. I can't make the payments. We can stay here till we lose everything," he'd said, "or we can sell now for what we can get. It won't be much. Maybe enough to pay our debts. Maybe not."

"But what would you do?" Holding tight to the edge of the kitchen table, she sank down on a chair.

"Try to get a job at the garage."

He was good with engines, with anything mechanical. Hadn't he kept that old Ford going all these years? And he was always taking off down the road to repair some neighbor's machinery.

She had clutched at his shirt. "One more year, Martin, one more year? I'm only thirty-seven." She'd thought that she had a lifetime to fill herself up with the farm. "Something will come up."

"That's what we said last year."

"We don't need much. Look at all the food I put up from the garden every summer. We'll get by."

"We're not making enough from the crops to pay for the seed. You know that."

"But the old folks are buried here. We're going to be buried here, aren't we?" Tears blinded her. "You promised," she cried, wringing the hem of her apron as if it were wet laundry.

He hung his head and stumbled to the door.

Later, she washed her face at the kitchen pump and went out to the garden. Lying down between rows of beans, she closed her eyes against the sun and clung to the straw beneath. She was in danger of falling off the planet.

When she opened her eyes, a man in a gray fedora and three-piece business suit was standing over her.

Sweeping the hat from his head, he said, "Mrs. Drew? I've come about the farm."

But why was she thinking about losing the farm? It really had nothing to do with Harriet.

Yet the past has a will of its own, and you must learn to entertain it, because it will visit, invited or not.

CHAPTER 16

Bess

BESS WOKE AT SEVEN, and was bathed and dressed by a quarter past. Dashing downstairs, she heard Aunt Kate and Harriet in the kitchen washing dishes. That was unusual. Ordinarily they didn't cook a big breakfast on weekdays.

No time to stop. She would phone Kate from work after the early rush. Flying out the front door, she called, "See you later," and ran most of the way to the Loon Cafe, a deep, narrow building sandwiched between the Majestic Theater and Mather's Five and Dime.

At the end of this same block was the *Standard Ledger* and above it Hanlon Land and Investments, where, in an hour or so, Doyle Hanlon would assist his father at dabbling in futures. Would he show up bleary and slow after his late night? Would Herbert Hanlon ask how he'd come by those dark circles under his eyes and advise him to stay home at night?

That home which he shared with a wife named Jean, and twin boys whose names Bess did not know, was out by the Navarins' on North End Road. Houses along that unpaved street were set on half acre and acre lots carved from farmland twenty years ago. Many, like the Navarins', had orchards. Bess could not recall whether Doyle Hanlon's house had apple trees. Amazing, the things you didn't notice when you hadn't a reason.

Herbert and Rebecca Hanlon lived in a substantial old house with broad porches on Catalpa Street, a block from the tiny clapboard Episcopal church where Rebecca Hanlon was a leading light. Bess tried to recall when the Episcopalians had their bazaar. Wasn't it around Thanksgiving? If she were home from college then, she would tag along with Aunt Kate and Harriet, and make it a point to buy something Doyle Hanlon's mother had made.

Perhaps she and Mrs. Hanlon would strike up a conversation. Bess rebuked herself for the several ignored opportunities she had had in the past for talking with that lady. Had she chatted with her at a bazaar, she might know some important or even negligible details of Doyle Hanlon's history. But what could be negligible?

Home from college. Going away to school had overnight lost its appeal. She wasn't considering changing her mind about college, of course. And naturally she wasn't considering meeting Doyle Hanlon at the Lucky Club.

When she'd awakened at seven, a fist-size lump of guilt had lain in her stomach, a heaviness she'd never known before. It was still there, weighing her down, and wouldn't go away until she told Doyle that she couldn't meet him.

Despite her resolve, Bess knew that she would love Doyle Hanlon as long as she lived. She could do nothing about that. Shuddering, she lay a hand on her midsection, where the stone of guilt lay.

Dora was in the kitchen heating the grill while her sixteen-year-old niece Shirley filled sugar dispensers. Dora glanced at the clock behind the counter as Bess rushed in. Seven twenty-eight. Bess was two minutes early. Dora liked that, and Bess wanted to please her. When she came home for summer vacation, she wanted to work at the Loon Cafe, at least part-time. She would need the money.

Snatching an apron from under the counter, suddenly Bess stood unmoving, the garment halfway to her waist—unless Doyle Hanlon moved away, Christ forbid, he would be in the Loon Cafe and the Lucky Club, at the Dakota Ballroom and elsewhere when she came home from college. How could she endure it? How, for that matter, could she endure the next couple of weeks, catching sight of him in his car or, worse, waiting on him in the cafe? She could stop going to the Lucky, but she couldn't quit her job.

Wrapping the apron around her waist with slow-motion attention to each detail, she stared at the Coca-Cola calendar on the wall behind the counter. Wasn't it fortunate that she hadn't met Doyle Hanlon sooner? She would already have suffered the loss of him.

"Back booths!" Dora yelled at her.

Bess grabbed an order pad from beside the cash register and stuck a pencil in her hair. Breakfast was busy. Bess and Shirley ran back and forth from counter to booths to kitchen. Shirley was a good waitress—not very smart, but she had the routine down. She knew the menu backward and forward, and she knew what could be special-ordered and what couldn't. She could even quote prices for banquets and gala occasions. Shirley took pride in being more restaurant wise than Bess. Bess might be going off to St. Cloud Teachers College, but she, Shirley, could handle four booths and the counter during a busy lunch, while Bess had trouble with two booths and the counter.

After the breakfast rush, Bess and Shirley were supposed to busy themselves with "housekeeping." This morning Dora handed Bess a stack of old newspapers and a bottle of ammonia.

"The front window's all flyspecked."

Bess was standing on the wide ledge inside the window where Dora displayed handbills for the Dakota Ballroom and the St. Bridget County Fair. Embarrassed to be on display herself, Bess hoped that Doyle Hanlon wouldn't choose this moment to stop in for coffee. If he did, Shirley would get to wait on him. Shirley was sitting at the counter, although Dora had told her to clean the toilets.

At ten-thirty Donna climbed onto a revolving stool at the counter and spun around, perky as hell, like Betty Garrett in *On the Town*, and ordered a Coke from Shirley, who scurried to wait on her. Donna was a favorite of Shirley's. Not only was she a graduating senior, pretty and popular, but she took the time to discuss movie stars and their clothes. Looking immaculate and innocent in jeans and a freshly ironed white blouse, Donna told Bess, "Jack Comstock's in front of Anderson's, watching you."

Bess craned. Yes, there he was, lounging on the front fender of Sherman Worley's Plymouth and flashing her an imbecilic grin.

Giving the window a final swipe with the crumpled newspaper, Bess hopped down. "There's no law against looking," she observed.

"You wouldn't give him another chance?" Donna asked.

"I wouldn't give him the time of day."

This was the sort of thing Shirley wanted to hear, the kind of exciting seventeen-year-old talk she longed to be part of.

Bess did not like discussing anything personal in front of Shirley, who was all ears and no brain. "You got home all right last night?" she asked Donna.

"Oh, sure."

"What did you think of your escort?" She did not say "Bob Arliss," because it was none of Shirley's business.

"He's all right."

"Will you go out with him again?"

Donna played with her straw and blew bubbles in the Coke. "I don't know. He's very sweet and a good dancer, but he didn't go to college."

Three men came in for coffee, settling into the front booth. Since Bess's hands were full of ammonia and wadded newspaper, Shirley took the order.

Quickly Donna asked, "What about *you* last night?"

"I got home fine, just fine. No problems." Bess turned away to dispose of the newspaper. "I'll be right back. I have to wash my hands."

Bess had never lied to Donna. She hadn't actually lied to her now, but she'd implied something which wasn't true, namely that Doyle Hanlon had brought her immediately home from the Dakota.

In the ladies' restroom, which had formerly been a closet and was large enough for only one person, Bess studied herself in the crazed mirror and wondered how much Donna would know simply by looking at her. Was it written on her face that she was in love with a married man? Did guilt flush in her cheeks?

Donna was perceptive. Would she be hurt or angry if she saw that Bess was lying? Bess sat down on the toilet and held her head. If she sensed that Donna was going to break off their friendship, she would have to break it off first. She wasn't sure how, since Donna hadn't *done* anything, but she would find an excuse.

Should she tell Donna about Doyle? But, Christ, loving a married man was a scandal. Donna was bound to be revolted. Even if Bess swore that she was not going to see him again, Donna might be uncomfortable with their friendship. Guilt by association, or something like that. Would everyone turn against her if they knew that she loved Doyle Hanlon? *Well, of course they would.*

"There's customers!" Dora was pounding on the door.

"Sorry," Bess muttered, unlocking the door and hurrying out. "I felt sick."

"There's a whole lot of coffee-breakers out there. Too many for Shirley to handle. Get sick later."

The counter was filled and nearly all of the booths had a couple of customers. Most of them only wanted coffee and a doughnut or roll, but they were in a hurry. Unless they were bosses, they only had fifteen minutes.

Bess and Shirley flew back and forth while Dora ran the cash register. Within minutes things were under control.

"I'm sorry," Bess told Dora. She could not afford to lose her job.

"You getting your period?" Dora inquired under her breath.

"I think so."

"You got pads?"

"Yes, thanks."

Donna was still at the counter. "Doyle Hanlon came in while you were washing your hands. He was looking around for someone. I guess he didn't find them because he left."

Since yesterday, life was dense with inference. Bess's hands shook and she stuffed them into the pockets of her apron. Was Donna implying something?

And Doyle, what had become of him? He'd probably gone back to work, assuming that she was avoiding him, that she was sorry she'd let him kiss her.

"I wonder who he was looking for," Bess said.

"Maybe Earl Ingbretson."

"Probably."

"I have to get home and help my mom shampoo the living room rug. I'll talk to you later. What time do you get off?"

"Three-thirty."

The lunch crowd began trickling in around eleven-thirty. By noon the place was full and several people were clustered by the door, waiting. Business hadn't been this hectic in weeks. Although it was too much work for three, especially with Dora fry-cooking, Bess was grateful to have no time to think about Doyle Hanlon. She whipped about, handling the counter and two booths, but also filling fountain orders and making sandwiches. Both she and Shirley had to run the cash register.

At a quarter to one Harriet and Rose turned up. Normally Harriet carried a lunch pail to the Water and Power Company, and Rose ate at the Friendship Arms Nursing Home, where she worked. What was the occasion? Bess wondered.

Harriet was spiffed up, wearing a shell-pink sleeveless dress of linenlike fabric, which she had worn only to church and to Bess's graduation early in June. On her wrist was a Black Hills gold bracelet, which she never wore to work. Maybe they were meeting some other women for a luncheon party, a baby or bridal shower. If so, Bess knew nothing about it and they hadn't arranged it with Dora.

As the two women sailed past, headed for an empty booth, Harriet smiled benevolently in all directions and wafted Shalimar, her special-occasions scent, onto the hamburger-reeking afternoon. Rose winked at Bess. "Wait'll you hear the news."

Shirley was servicing the far booths and Bess was running the cash register, so she had no opportunity to talk to Harriet until much later, when the lunch crowd petered out.

"Your cousin ordered T-bone," Shirley told Bess. "She must be celebrating." Maybe Harriet had gotten a promotion or a big raise.

At one-thirty Dora told Bess to take a break. "You girls have been running pretty hard the last couple of hours, and you with the curse." Dora was always in a good mood when the cafe was busy.

For lying about her period, God would probably send Bess really bad cramps next time. She shrugged and poured a tall glass of iced tea. Helping herself to two scoops of butter brickle ice cream, she carried her lunch back to Harriet and Rose's booth.

"Hello, little girl," Harriet said, moving over to make room for Bess. "Dora give you a break?"

Bess nodded. "You're all dolled up," she observed, scraping small spoonfuls of ice cream, savoring each as though it were individual and slightly different from the others. "Did you get a raise or something?"

Harriet and Rose were eating cherry pie à la mode. Harriet finished hers and wiped her mouth on the paper napkin. Nearly all her lipstick came off, and she was suddenly colorless and vulnerable. Bess was touched. Hardworking and brave and laughable Harriet. And loyal.

Rose stood. "Excuse me, ladies. Nature calls." As Rose walked away, Harriet said, "I saw you at the Dakota last night."

Oh God, here it comes, Bess thought.

"Yes," Bess said. "I was going to say hi, but I couldn't find you."

"It was so hot. I got a little overheated and went outside."

Bess nodded.

"Were you with Doyle Hanlon and Earl Ingbretson?"

"I got a ride with them. I wasn't *with* them."

"You seemed to be dancing a lot with Doyle Hanlon."

"I didn't know many people."

"Some people might think the wrong thing, seeing you dancing so many numbers with the same man. A married man."

"They'd be wrong," Bess lied.

"You and I know that, but people are quick to criticize. You don't want to get a bad name."

"Of course not." Throughout this little conversation, Bess's pulse pounded so hard, she wondered if Harriet couldn't see it in her temple and down the side of her neck. She kept her eyes on the butter brickle ice cream and concentrated on speaking with a calm, disinterested voice.

"I didn't mention Doyle Hanlon to Kate," Harriet told her.

"Thanks, Harriet." Bess scooped up a spoonful of candy-studded ice cream and held it to Harriet's mouth. "Try this. It's really good."

When Harriet had swallowed the ice cream and again wiped her mouth, she began to play nervously with her coffee spoon. She smiled what seemed a pointless smile. Must be something to do with the promotion, Bess thought.

"I want to tell you something before Rose comes back," Harriet launched. "I hope it will make you happy, because you're like a daughter to me. I've never said that, but I've felt it. And I think you've felt it."

Bess nodded.

Harriet's eyes were misty and her long nose was red, as if she was about to cry. Bess put an arm across the woman's shoulders.

"What is it, Harriet? What can be so wonderful if it upsets you?" Suddenly Bess knew what. Her belly froze and stiffened against the news.

"I'm getting married."

Slowly, her arm prickling with revulsion, Bess withdrew it, hugging it to herself.

"Last night DeVore Weiss asked me to marry him and I said yes." For the second time that day, Harriet wept. "Please don't be angry, Bess."

"Don't be angry?"

"I can see that you're angry."

"I don't understand you, Harriet," Bess heard herself say coldly. "You're always calling yourself an old maid. Don't you see, that's what you're *supposed* to be. Now you're going to make a fool of yourself, marrying some stupid clodhopper who's looking for a cheap hired girl. Well, go right ahead. Go right ahead. Mother a houseful of morons. They can probably use a hired girl to clean up after them, but don't come telling me how much you love me, because I'll never believe you."

With some dignity Harriet told her, "He isn't a stupid clodhopper, and his children aren't morons."

They faced each other for a moment, before Bess shoved the metal ice cream dish, sending it careering across the table and onto the seat where Rose had been sitting. Flinging herself away, Bess nearly knocked Rose down. Her face burned with hatred and injury. She would not cry. And she wouldn't hang around where Harriet could see her.

In the kitchen Dora was surprised to see Bess plunge into the stacks of dirty dishes. "Here," she said, "put on a bigger apron. You'll need it."

Bess couldn't believe that Harriet was marrying DeVore Weiss. It wasn't a thing that could be envisioned. But, at the same time, she *did* envision it, and she was nauseated: Harriet embracing DeVore's children, his two little girls, much younger than Bess.

It was that damned business with Dixie all over again, only much worse, because this time Harriet really *was* leaving. Scrubbing away the pinkish goo of cherry pie à la mode, Bess thrust the plate deep into the big cast-iron sink, seeing in the dirty dishwater a bleak landscape of desertion.

The temperature was about a hundred degrees in the kitchen. Perspiration ran down Bess's face and fell from her nose and chin into the dishwater, but her insides were frozen, just as they had been nine years ago when the damnable, curly-headed moppet from Mason City had shown up.

At two-thirty, when the coffee-break customers flocked in again, Bess hung upon their casual remarks and lingered over their orders, as if the warm juices of human contact might drive both DeVore Weiss and Dixie away.

But when the customers were gone, Bess felt false and empty. Hungry for something indefinable, something that Dora didn't serve in the Loon Cafe. She returned to the steaming sink and white dishes, from each of which Dixie's face smiled out triumphantly.

CHAPTER 17

Harriet

"DON'T TELL THEM you have a dentist's appointment!" Kate had cried with impatience. "Tell them you're engaged and you're taking the day off."

That was the advice that Harriet wanted to hear, and she called the Water and Power Company, warbling into the receiver, "I'm an engaged woman!"

Martha had answered the phone, and she of course hollered the news to the rest of the office, and all the girls had gotten on the line to congratulate Harriet and inquire when the happy day was to be. To each Harriet confided that she didn't know, since it had all happened out of the blue and she and DeVore hadn't talked about dates. She hoped by tomorrow to be able to inform them. She could count on them for a bridal shower, they assured her, and Harriet hung up pleased and as pink as her crinkle-cotton robe.

Being affianced was good for Harriet's complexion, rouging her cheeks with satisfaction, even plumping out her figure a little, she liked to think. Of course, she'd packed away two hearty meals between 2:00 and 6:00 A.M.

Next she rang Rose at the Friendship Arms Nursing Home. Rose was away from her desk. "I'll wait," Harriet told the person on the line. "I've got plenty of time." She sat at Kate's desk, legs crossed, swinging her free leg restlessly. She might have plenty of time, but she was nearly wetting her pants to tell Rose the news.

"Rose! Guess what!" But then she was overcome with glee and couldn't talk. She made little squealing, mouse noises, laughing between each and ending up with hiccoughs. When she was composed enough to speak coherently, each sentence was punctuated by a hiccough. Eventually she and Rose were laughing too hard to talk, so they hung up, and Harriet, still hiccoughing, went upstairs to luxuriate in her new well-being.

Harriet gave herself a manicure and pedicure and applied a rosy-pink polish to all twenty nails. When she had plucked her eyebrows, she shaved her legs. It was too late to do anything about her hair. If she washed it, it would never dry in time for lunch, especially with the air so humid. She would spray it with cologne and roll it up while she took her bath. The combination of steam and cologne, she had read somewhere, would put a little body back in your hair when you didn't have time to get to the hairdresser. Not that Harriet often went to the hairdresser. Two or three times a year for a cut and permanent. She'd tried a Toni home perm once, and for two months afterward looked like a dishwater-blond Orphan Annie.

For half an hour she lay dreaming in the bath. She supposed that DeVore would want to be married in the winter since it was hard to leave a farm in the summer, even with a couple of teenage sons still at home to help. A holiday wedding was in some ways more romantic than a June wedding, Harriet thought.

Maybe they would drive to Florida for a honeymoon, or maybe they'd stay home and celebrate with the children. There would be Christmas presents to buy, a tree to trim, cookies to bake, and she was sure to discover little changes she wanted to make in the house right away, to put her own stamp on it.

On second thought, it might be better to wait until after Christmas to be married. DeVore's wife had passed away last December. December would be a sad anniversary for him and the children. And wouldn't a Valentine's wedding be the most romantic of all? In her own mind, Harriet decided on Valentine's Day. *Six months.*

When she was downtown this afternoon she would stop by Egger's Drugstore and pick up a couple of bride magazines. She wasn't intending to have a splashy affair with a long veil and train and all of that. For a woman her age it would not be in good taste. But she did want to treat herself to the finest wedding a thirty-nine-year-old woman could tastefully enjoy.

Back in her bedroom, she stood in her slip surveying the open closet. One by one she pulled dresses out, held them up to herself in front of the bureau mirror, and rejected them. At length she chose the shell pink. Ladylike, but quite stylish. It had an engagement look to it. She set it aside. No point in putting it on yet. It would only wrinkle.

Standing before the mirror, Harriet studied her form. Her shoulders were sharp, as were her elbows and hips, but she had a bosom. She wouldn't exchange her 32B for all the rounded hips and plump arms in southern Minnesota.

If DeVore had wanted a round woman, he wouldn't have taken up with her.

She was a little nervous, though, about his seeing her with her clothes off. Would he tease her about her . . . slimness? Would he find, in bed, that she had too many corners?

She lay down across the smoothly stretched candlewick bedspread. She had so much to think about, most of it pleasant, but some of it worrisome. What would DeVore look like with his clothes off? Would he want to sleep with her now that they were engaged? And if he did, *where*? She herself looked forward to that aspect of the future, but she did not want to appear too eager. He might think he'd gotten himself a floozy. On the other hand, she didn't want him to think she was frigid. Would he break off the engagement for either reason? Her only sharp fear was that he would find a reason to break off with her. The engagement was too new to trust. If she were young and pretty, it would be different. Whatever she might tell Rose, she did not consider herself a catch.

Beside the bed, on the lower shelf of her bedside table, Harriet kept a stack of *Better Homes and Gardens* she'd been saving in case she ever got married. She had never seen the inside of DeVore's house, but she had an idea that it would need plenty of clever fixing up of the sort described in the pages of *Better Homes and Gardens*.

She was fairly handy with a sewing machine and owned her own Singer portable, so she could zip up curtains and slipcovers economically. With curtains and slipcovers and a coat of paint, you could transform the dreariest rooms, creating cozy, stylish surroundings for family and friends.

As she lay across the bed, Harriet's mood turned blue with old regret, and she rolled onto her side and curled into a ball. If only her parents had lived to see what she'd made of herself. Ten years they'd been dead, and she was still trying to please them.

They had not approved of girls. Girls were trouble. Girls were sly, silly, scheming, weak-bodied, weak-minded, monthly bleeding parasites. Girls put on hoity-toity airs and were ungrateful. They thought they were better than their families.

Boys, on the other hand, were strong and loyal and down to earth. They looked you in the eye and gave you an honest day's work. Never mind that Billy and Jesse were cunning and lazy and cruel. Harriet's parents translated their flaws into virtues. Their cunning was cleverness; their sloth, easiness; their cruelty, toughness. Harriet could not win.

The boys were three and five years older than Harriet. When she graduated from business college, Billy was selling women's shoes in a cheap chain store. Jesse was night clerk at the Clark Hotel. Harriet had invited her parents and the boys to a celebration dinner at the Country Cottage Restaurant. Explaining to the manager that she was celebrating business-college graduation with her family, Harriet had ordered the meal ahead of time, choosing everyone's favorite dishes.

Dinner started with fruit cup, followed by prime rib

and french fried potatoes, baby peas and Parker House rolls. She had not preordered dessert, as she was unsure whether the boys would prefer apple or blueberry pie à la mode. When the dinner plates were cleared away and the moment arrived for dessert and coffee, the waitress carried in a small cake, holding it dramatically aloft. Setting it before Harriet, she sang out, "Congratulations, Harriet."

The cake was decorated with tiny pink roses, graceful garlands, and a rolled sheepskin tied with a pink ribbon. The waitress's "Congratulations, Harriet" was repeated in flowing script that curlicued across the top.

"Oh my word," Harriet gasped. "It's beautiful." Tears filled her eyes. Billy and Jesse despised her occasional tears, so she hastily dabbed them with her napkin. She did not want to spoil the party.

"Would you like me to cut it?" the waitress asked. They all had a big piece, and plenty was left over to take home.

"Thank you," Harriet told her parents and brothers when the waitress had left. "That was the prettiest cake I ever saw."

"*We* didn't order it," her mother said with heavy-footed indignation. With times so hard, did Harriet imagine that *they* could indulge in expensive folderol? She put her arm through the strap of her large black handbag. She was missing *One Man's Family* on the radio.

"It wasn't us," Billy told her, looking at his brother and laughing. "Ah, Harriet, you ordered it yourself. Come on, admit it. Who else'd be ordering a fancy cake like that for an old-maid business lady?"

"Well, *someone* ordered it for me," Harriet protested, "because *I* didn't."

Then they were all laughing at her, convinced that she'd ordered the cake, that she wanted them to believe she had a secret admirer. The boys wouldn't let up, but were still at her about it as they all prepared to leave.

Harriet sent them ahead while she paid the bill and left the tip. The waitress who was clearing the table told her, "The cake was a little surprise from the management. We hope you enjoyed it."

Harriet never told her family that the restaurant had given her the cake. She couldn't bear to hear another word about it. That night she decided to visit Cousin Kate in Harvester. Maybe she would find work in Minnesota. Harriet sent Christmas cards to her brothers but never heard from them.

She uncurled her long body and sat up. Time to get dressed and put on her makeup. She looked around at the pink-and-white room she would be leaving in February. She had had a good life here, and she would have a good life with DeVore. She would be a prizewinning wife and homemaker, entering homemade watermelon pickles and baked items in the county fair and making her husband proud. DeVore would have no reason to regret having asked for her.

Whatever the battle had been between herself and her own family, she had won it.

CHAPTER 18

Kate

HARRIET AND ROSE HAD DRIVEN OFF in Harriet's car, laughing and prattling on about Rose and someone named Ernie. Over and over Harriet had said, "You'll be next, Rose. Mark my words. You'll be next."

Kate had followed them out to the front sidewalk to see them off, smiling and waving. She must not appear saddened by Harriet's engagement. She must not rob the woman of her blind happiness. Blind happiness was not a thing you could hang on to, nor would you want to, really, but it was something everyone deserved—Harriet more than most—once or twice in a lifetime.

Soon enough, being Harriet, she would begin to worry. About winning over DeVore's children, about keeping a man happy year in and year out, about leaving Kate alone, and worst, perhaps, about losing Bess. In some sense, Bess was the only child of her own that Harriet would ever have. If, as Harriet said, she and Rose were having lunch at the Loon Cafe, Harriet's blind happiness could be lost in the next hour.

Kate had tried to talk Harriet and Rose into driving over to St. Bridget and having lunch at the St. Bridget Hotel, where the steaks were said to be excellent. On the way back they could have swung around by Red Berry and picked up Rose's car at the Dakota Ballroom, but Harriet had insisted on the Loon Cafe. Kate supposed that Harriet wanted to dine where the greatest number of people who knew her would witness her brand-new state of engagement. Had she truly not foreseen what might happen when Bess heard the news?

Kate climbed the front steps, leaning heavily on the cane. She must invite DeVore and his children to dinner. A week from Sunday, maybe. Whatever they were like, they must be welcomed and made to feel a part of Harriet's family. Kate was not acquainted with the Weisses, who lived east of town, except by name. They couldn't be too bad or she'd have heard something. And who was she to pass judgment, she with Celia and Archer still grist for the mill? If only Bess would mind herself when the Weisses came to dinner, if only she would not run off someplace, refusing to accept them, or, worse, hang about with her smart mouth.

The rules and boundaries Bess set were so personal, so much based on her own private losses and fears, that no one else could fully understand them or even know when they were transgressing them.

Sitting on the stool by the kitchen window, Kate watched the purple grackles in the driveway, squawking and fighting over the toast scraps she'd tossed out for the robins. She didn't like grackles. They were aggressive dispossessors.

But they were what they were, she supposed. They took

what they wanted. Like the man in the fedora—though he had not squawked, but had spoken in refined and businesslike tones. No one had ever spoken to her in tones quite so civil.

She glanced away from the window and began slicing a peach into sections, laying the sections on a plate, while her thoughts returned to Bess. However irrational the child was, she was theirs, hers and Harriet's.

Kate spread a slice of bread with peanut butter, cut it into two pieces, and laid them on either side of the peach. How pretty the brown was against the golden fruit.

The front screen door squeaked. "Kate?"

"In the kitchen, Frieda."

"I've got the car outside. I'm on my way to Truska's. Can I get you something? Would you like to come?"

Kate began eating the peach slices. They were sweet and fine textured, and she was grateful to have tasted them at their best moment. "Are you in a hurry?"

"No. Take your time. You don't eat enough. What do you weigh, ninety-five pounds?"

"I meant, would you have a little time—"

"To drive in the country?"

Kate laughed. "You should go into the mind-reading business."

"It's not hard to read *your* mind. You always want to go for a drive in the country."

"Do I? Yes, you're probably right."

"We'll go for a little drive first, and then we'll go shop. That way the butter won't melt before we get home."

Kate finished the peach and placed a small Pyrex bowl over the bread and peanut butter to keep it fresh for later. "I'll just get my purse," she said.

"It's a pity they had to run that item about the accident in yesterday's paper," Frieda observed as Kate fetched her purse. "I didn't want to mention it in front of Marie Wall last night, but I was provoked, and I rang 'em at the paper and said as much. You know what they said? They said they needed colorful items that would be of interest to their readers, and not much was happening ten years ago this week. I said, 'What about World War Two?'"

"It was good of you to ring them, Frieda, but you didn't need to. We don't have to worry about them running it again for another ten years." She put the purse strap over her wrist and took down a straw hat from the hook beside the back door. She needed to get out into the fresh air.

Climbing in and out of the car was more and more difficult, but she would do it as long as she was able. She regretted never learning to drive, and she was glad that Bess had learned at school. Rides in the country made Kate feel unaccountably young and uncrippled.

When she was settled in the front seat beside Frieda, Kate pulled a silk scarf from her purse, and because her fingers were stiff, Frieda tied it around her head to keep her hair from flying all over when the wind blew through the window. She would put on the hat when they got to the farm.

Her heart flew out the window and across the fields, some of them as deeply green as the inside of a jungle, others as soft and golden as the down of baby chicks. The smells of clover and newly mown grass lifted her high, high, high until she was beside herself with pleasure, seeing life from a great height. No wonder birds seemed so recklessly happy. Flight put things into perspective.

Big, strong hands at ten o'clock and two o'clock on the steering wheel, Frieda drove with resolute concentration but without conspicuous fear, as if the car were a skittish team of horses known for kicking over the traces, but she, Frieda, was a match for them. At the edge of town she turned onto the gravel road and headed north.

The great, flapping corn leaves waved to Kate and she waved back in the manner of royalty, riding out among her subjects, loving and blessing them all. When she died she wished that she could be buried in someone's cornfield or under a stand of country trees like those old oaks ahead. She had once thought that she would be buried by the grove on the farm, next to the old folks.

A mile farther on she said, "Frieda, could we—"

"Stop for a minute?"

Kate glanced askance at Frieda. The woman had a knack for anticipating. She was like the faithful dog who lopes to the door just as you're thinking you might want a walk.

Slowing, Frieda turned off the road and into a barely discernible drive, much overgrown, which led through barbed-wire fencing whose jury-rigged gate was left open. Shifting into low gear, she passed an ABSOLUTELY NO HUNTING OR TRESPASSING sign, sniffed and "hmmphed" as if to say, "Some nerve," then proceeded alongside the box elder grove on her left, nearly impenetrable with fallen trees, saplings, and undergrowth.

The car bounced in the ruts, and the long grass hissed against its undercarriage. Dust filtered up, and Kate held her hand out the window as if to catch the rising dust and the thick, hot sunlight beating down on it.

Veering left, Frieda pulled into a clearing where an old house stood and, some distance from it, a barn lay like a collapsed Chinese lantern.

Kate saw Martin coming in from the fields, sweat and black dirt painting a map of work on his face and neck and arms, saw herself running to meet him and slipping away with him for a few minutes to lie down in the grove.

Stopping the car before the broad front porch of the house, Frieda turned off the ignition. The high, whining whirr of cicadas, like the sound of a dentist's drill, rushed to fill the void. Ahead, where the car pointed, was a second grove, this one cottonwoods, and beyond it lay a pond.

For several minutes the two women sat in silence, Frieda plucking a handkerchief from her bosom and polishing her dusty eyeglasses while Kate studied the house with a pitying and devouring eye.

The house sagged along the roofline like a swaybacked horse. Gingerbread was missing from the eaves. But the kitchen's tin chimney glinted in the sunlight as if it were new.

Though intact, the windows were dark and unwashed. They gazed out with a sadness lacking all hope. Kate's body clenched with an anger old but still strong.

Frieda reached into the glove compartment for a small

paper bag and said, "Let's get out. Put on your hat." Opening her door, Frieda waded around the car through weeds that grabbed at her cotton stockings, pinning prickly seeds to them.

Leaning on her cane and with Frieda holding her other arm, Kate picked her way through the snarled growth of foxtail and knotweed, bindweed and pigweed, bearing toward that spot down nearly to the cottonwoods. Her ankles throbbed like aching teeth.

As they approached, Frieda dispersed a swarm of gnats, fanning at them with her own broad straw hat. The little wooden crosses were long gone, rotted to splinters. But, yes, the rocks were there, outlining the two graves. Why was it that she always expected them to be gone?

Standing beside the graves, Kate apologized to the old folks as she always did when she came here. At her elbow, Frieda clasped her hands together in a moment of reverence. What a good woman Frieda was, Kate thought.

"Stay here a minute," Frieda told her. "I'm gonna pick you some woodruff."

That was what the little bag was for, Kate realized. Woodruff for headache tea. "It's up next to the house on the north side."

Returning, Frieda saw that Kate was weak. Perspiration was running down the sides of her face, dripping from her jaw onto the deep rose of her dress. Frieda steered her around, back toward the car, assuring her, "Next time we'll walk down to the pond."

Panting, Kate wheezed, "I used to leap across the creek, you know . . ." she breathed raggedly ". . . where it squeezes out into the pasture." Her lips screwed into a smile. You could tell a dear friend something important again and again, knowing they would not mind the repetition.

"You felt like you could fly," Frieda supplied.

"That's right. Blind happiness. That was my blind happiness."

Back in the car, when she had caught her breath and wiped her brow with a handkerchief, she told Frieda, "Harriet is engaged."

"Engaged! Who to?"

"DeVore Weiss. He farms east of town."

"His mother was an Apel."

"I didn't know that."

"I don't know the Weisses, but the Apels were good people, hard workers, all of them."

"He asked her last night after the dance."

"I hope it wasn't the whiskey talking."

"No. From what Harriet said, he was perfectly sober. He took her to the all-night for a steak dinner first."

Frieda laughed. "Needed to get his strength up."

"He never even asked her home from the dance before, then all of a sudden he pops the question."

"Maybe he just wants his way with her."

"No. I think he's serious. She asked if she could put it in the paper. He said she could put it on the radio."

"Well, he's got a sense of humor."

"Yes."

"That's important. I couldn't stand a man that didn't have a sense of humor, even if he was a hard worker." Pulling onto the county road again, Frieda said, "You'll miss

Harriet. She's a good girl. A little silly and puts on airs, but she's a hard worker and loyal. She appreciates family, coming from such a bunch of bums as she had to live with. My, but those brothers of hers was dumb clucks. Mean, too. Harriet got all the sense in that family."

"Yes."

"But listen to me! Heavens, she's only going out to the country, not to Des Moines."

"I know. I know."

"Still, things will be different. They're bound to be," Frieda observed.

"The beginning of my old age," Kate said and hoped that it didn't sound too self-pitying. "Harriet and Bess have kept me young."

"Pish-posh."

"With both of them gone, I'll be an old lady."

"Then you and me'll be old ladies together."

Too soon, town was before them, the country behind. At the edge of Harvester, where they made a right turn, a dark-blue car coming from town was heading into the country.

"The girl in that car reminded me of Bess."

"What car?"

"A dark-blue one, back where we turned."

"I didn't see."

Only a glimpse. The girl's hair was pulled back in a ponytail. But then many girls wore their hair that way. Kate wished that she'd gotten a closer look, at the girl and at the driver. Funny how a glimpse from a distance, like a familiar scent on the air, could set you to remembering. And worrying.

CHAPTER 19

Bess

BESS DRIED THE WATER GLASSES, setting them on a tray to be carried out to the counter. Of course it was wrong, she thought, to feel the way she did toward Harriet, to say the things she'd said. Her anger was a loyal black beast that devoured friends and enemies, protecting her from them. Though she wasn't really sure who had been devoured when Dixie had come to visit.

Bess had been eight when Dixie showed up with her mother. Dixie's mother, Alda, a cousin of Uncle Martin's (though he was dead by this time), had driven up from Mason City, Iowa. She and Dixie were on their way to Minneapolis for a wedding. They'd started out early in order to spend a couple of days with Kate. Bess remembered thinking that Dixie was a dumb name for a little girl from Iowa.

Three years younger than Bess, Dixie still had the curving, dimpled shape of a small child, and she had a head of soft, natural curls. She put some people in mind of a cherub.

First gazing on Dixie, Harriet had exclaimed, "Shirley Temple. She looks just like Shirley Temple. Kate, doesn't she look just like Shirley Temple in *Wee Willie Winkie*?"

back to her own room, Bess sat down on the floor and cut the soft fabric into small pieces, which fell to the floor around her like flower petals.

When she was done, she didn't know what to do with the pieces. Searching in the back of her closet, she dug out an old shoe box and stuffed them into that, burying the box under a pile of dirty clothes. Exhausted, she climbed into bed and fell asleep.

Much later, Harriet came into Bess's room and woke her to inquire if she'd seen Dixie's dress. Bess shook her head.

"You must have. It didn't get up and walk away."

"Maybe she put it somewhere and forgot."

"No, she didn't. Alda says the dress was on their suitcase when Dixie left for the movies. Tell me the truth now, where is it?"

"I don't know," Bess said, sticking out her lower lip and glaring at Harriet.

Aunt Kate had appeared in the doorway. "Look in her closet, Harriet."

"You stay out of my closet. Those are my things in there!" Bess shouted.

Alda and Dixie were crowding into the room, Dixie in her nightgown, tears staining her face. Bess pulled herself up, backbone pressed hard against the headboard. Would Alda call Constable Wall and have her arrested?

Harriet was going through Bess's clothes, which were on hangers, searching to see if the dress was hidden there. Dixie had set up a real tune. You could probably hear her over at Frieda's, but Bess didn't take her eyes off the closet door.

Finally Harriet emerged with the shoe box, her face a study in disbelief. "How could you?" she asked again and again, as if she seriously expected an answer. She held the open box out for Aunt Kate and Alda to see the remains.

"Oh my God," Alda said, and Dixie threw herself on the floor in howling hysterics. "I'm afraid she'll get sick over this," Alda told Aunt Kate, dragging Dixie out of the room.

Harriet followed, trying to soothe Dixie. "It's all right, little Dixie, we'll get you another one, don't you worry."

Aunt Kate stood looking at Bess when the others had gone. Bess pulled the covers up tight around her neck and pressed herself against the headboard until her spine felt crushed. She caught her lower lip in her teeth and stopped breathing. She wished that Aunt Kate would say something about how many years Bess was going to have to work to pay for the dress, or even how sad it would be when Constable Wall came to take her to jail. But she only looked at Bess, then turned and left, closing the door behind her.

"Aunt Kate, don't go," Bess had screamed, but her great-aunt didn't come back.

After Dixie, Bess hadn't spoken to Harriet for six weeks. This time she would never speak to her. *Marry DeVore Weiss, you old fool. Now you're a ghost, like Celia.*

At three o'clock Doyle Hanlon opened the screen door of the Loon Cafe. Bess stood at a back booth, taking an order for Cokes. Afterward she was certain that she had felt Doyle's gaze on her back. The skin along her spine had risen in goose bumps.

He sat down in the first booth and she hurried to it, happy that Shirley was at the malted milk machine. He wore gray trousers and a white dress shirt; his tie was loosened and the top button of the shirt unbuttoned. He looked very handsome and a little shy, as if he'd been perfectly sure of himself until he'd seen her, and then was abashed. He played idly with the Select-O-Matic as Bess walked toward the booth, more frightened than he could possibly be.

"May I help you?" She felt weak and illusory now, like a wraith.

"I'll have coffee," he told her.

Hand trembling, Bess wrote an illegible "coffee" on the pad. "Anything else?"

"Not right now."

She turned away to fetch the coffee, wishing that it were good, which it wasn't.

"Not right now," he'd said. Her heart felt like a wild bird caught indoors, beating against first this window, then that. If she heard a million other voices but did not hear his for twenty years, and if he then spoke in the dark or over the telephone, she would know his voice from the million.

This illness was love. It had lain dormant in her from birth. All last night she had had a peculiar sense of recognition, as if before birth someone had pointed him out, saying, "This man. This is the one."

She carried the coffee with special care, slowly, as if bearing Communion wine. None must slop over, making a pool in the saucer, which might stain his clothes.

She was unable to look away from him.

"When are you off work?" he asked quietly.

"Three-thirty."

"Were you tired this morning?"

"No."

"Me either. I haven't been tired all day."

She could think of nothing clever to say, and he deserved witty phrases.

No one in the cafe was waiting to be served, so Bess remained beside his booth, having lost the knack of walking back across the room.

"Bess!" Dora. She was toting up receipts at the cash register.

"Excuse me." Bess went, not willingly, to see what Dora wanted.

"Shirley never got those toilets cleaned," Dora told Bess when she had finished making change. "She's a good little waitress, but she's not much good for anything else. Would you do the toilets and sinks? Check the towel dispensers while you're at it. I'll sweep out later."

"You want me to do them now?" Bess asked, hoping she misunderstood.

"You're off in twenty minutes. If you don't do them now, they're not gonna get done."

Bess smiled at Doyle Hanlon and shrugged as she headed toward the restrooms. Maybe customers would be using them and she would have to wait until later.

Both small rooms were empty. She worked as fast as she could, but toilet paper scraps and paper towels lay wadded everywhere. And in the ladies', someone had scrawled

"Help!" on the mirror with lipstick. If Bess didn't clean it up, Dora would have a fit. She fetched the Windex from the supply closet.

Despite the droning fans overhead, the restrooms were nearly as hot as the kitchen. In the speckly mirror of the ladies,' Bess saw that strands of hair were coming loose from her ponytail and hanging in strings around her face. Her skin looked greasy and her lipstick was smudged. I look like someone in an Erskine Caldwell novel, she thought.

She must tell Dora that the men's floor needed mopping. Bess was glad that Dora never asked her to mop the restrooms. The men's was particularly distasteful. *Women* sat down. However, the women also scattered toilet paper from here to Sunday, putting it on the seat to protect themselves from syphilis and crabs, and then letting it fall to the floor and get shuffled around.

She could have taken all of this with good grace if she hadn't been dragged away from Doyle Hanlon. When she returned the Windex to the supply room, she saw that his booth was empty, the table cleared.

"Time to hang up the apron," Dora told her, inclining her head toward the clock. Three thirty-five. "You've done a good day's work."

Bess carried her soiled apron to the kitchen hamper. "The floor in the men's is a mess," she told Dora, grabbing her clutch bag from beneath the counter. "It's going to need mopping." Dora deserved to mop the men's.

Bess had resolved not to see Doyle Hanlon. Now, here she was, half-silly with grief at losing a few minutes of his time.

Outside the cafe, she squinted at the empty somnolence of Main Street. People were home with the shades pulled, wiping the back of their necks with dampened handkerchiefs.

As she neared the *Standard Ledger*, she saw Herbert Hanlon in his white suit and Panama hat emerge from the doorway leading to Hanlon Land and Investments. A demigod who dabbled in futures, he stared down the street at her as she approached, then pulled sunglasses from a pocket and put them on, heading toward her.

He *knows*, Bess thought. He's going to confront me. She tried neither to look at him nor to look away as he drew near. And then he was past. But he had looked at her, something he had never done before. He knew.

Bess's pulse was racing and she wished that she were home. Everyone on the street knew, she was sure. Halfway home, Doyle Hanlon's dark-blue Mercury pulled up. He leaned across the front seat and called to her through the open window, "Give you a lift?"

She should say no. In the senior Hanlon's glance she had read warning. But neither his cautionary gaze nor her own best intentions were sufficient against the sound of Doyle Hanlon's voice. She opened the door and climbed in, smiling determinedly.

"I smell of hamburgers and french fries," she said. "Do you smell of futures?"

He grinned at her. Bess's delight was so keen, her ears buzzed.

"Do you have a little time?" he asked.

Where were the *no*s she'd so carelessly flung at boys

who'd asked for a date or boys who'd tried to unbutton her blouse?

"A little. But I have to be home for supper."

Doyle Hanlon drove out of town by the route he had taken the previous night. At the edge of town a car, returning from the country, turned right and away from them, but not before Bess recognized Frieda's.

"Oh," she said.

"Something wrong?"

"My cousin Frieda's car turned there at the intersection. Aunt Kate was in the front seat."

"Is that bad?"

"I don't know."

They were in the open country now, past the last houses straggling toward farmland, and he took her hand. "You haven't done anything wrong."

"I don't know." But she did know. The lump of culpability in her stomach had grown heavier. She had fallen in love with a married man, the father of twin boys. Not knowing what he had in mind, she was allowing him to drive her into the country. She was her father's daughter.

But maybe he would only drive. Maybe he didn't intend anything more than that. Maybe theirs was to be a platonic love, simple and painful.

When she speculated along these lines, she felt silly being so upset over an innocent drive on a hot afternoon. If he could read her thoughts, he'd laugh at her. If he had more than conversation in mind, he would surely have chosen one of the beautiful girls home from college. Bess was certain that any female who spent more than a few minutes in his company would fall in love.

He looked at her with a serious, almost sad expression and pulled her toward him on the seat. She did not resist.

"I don't know how to explain what I'm doing," he said. "I don't want to do anything that will make you unhappy."

He said nothing for a few minutes. She waited for him to continue. She had no idea what he would say, nor even quite what he had meant by what he'd already said.

"Last night at the Lucky when I asked you to dance, I didn't have anything in mind, except to dance. You were a cute girl, a bright kid. I thought it would be fun having a few dances. It'd be like high school again, dancing with a nice, innocent girl. All fun and no worry." He squeezed her shoulder as if to say, Do you see what a fool I am?

"But you weren't all bubblegummy and giggly. I was talking more than I've talked in a long time—about Korea and work and books and whatever the hell. And you listened so . . . carefully.

"By the time we left the Dakota, I couldn't wait to get rid of Earl. It didn't really matter if all we did was talk . . . or not talk, just ride."

They passed the box elder grove where they'd parked last night. They were coming to a gas station halfway to Ula. Doyle pulled the car into the drive but not up to the pumps.

"What kind of pop do you like?"

"Root beer," she told him.

When he returned he was carrying two cold, wet bottles

of root beer from the ice case. Climbing in behind the wheel, he said, "My car is my kingdom. A few special guests are allowed—Earl; my little boys, Bret and Roger; and you."

His little boys, Bret and Roger. The names pierced Bess's side. How dare she sit where his little boys sat? The dashboard clock said a quarter past four, not late enough for her to tell him, "I have to get home now."

So she was relieved when he turned the car back in the direction from which they'd come. A short ride and a bottle of pop. Pretty innocent. She breathed country air deep into her lungs and relaxed.

A mile down the road, Doyle swung the car onto a narrow, overgrown lane that you wouldn't notice unless you looked closely. A sign was nailed to a fence post: ABSOLUTELY NO HUNTING OR TRESPASSING. Hugging a grove of box elders, the car bounced heedlessly over deep ruts. Ahead and to the left lay a clearing where an old farmhouse, gray and withered, stood staring at their approach. A barn had long since fallen to its knees.

Ignoring the house, the Mercury inched along an even narrower path leading away through another grove—like the first, dense with undergrowth.

"Don't be afraid," he told her. "There's a pond out here where my dad and I come duck hunting. I wanted to show it to you. It's quiet and unspoiled." He cast a fond eye around him.

"The old man owns the land and it's posted against trespassers, but I took the lock off the gate when I came back from Korea. It felt like we were running a prison for birds." He snorted at this romanticism.

As the Mercury crawled through the shrubbery and saplings, their soft green arms reached out for it. Beneath the car, grasses brushed seductively along its belly, making intimate, sighing sounds. After a hundred yards of creeping forward in deep twilight, the car emerged onto a narrow grassy bank before which lay a pond.

A storm of birds flew up. Thick with weeds and abundant reeds, it was not a pond used for swimming, but for the protection of birds so that they might subsequently be killed.

Doyle cut the engine. The density of the afternoon quiet was startling and a little unnerving. They had left the known world and entered a place without a particle of familiarity, a place not found on any map.

"Nobody farms this land?" Bess asked.

He shook his head and snapped the nail of his index finger against a bunch of keys hanging on a ring from the ignition. Among them was a silvery disc with the raised letter *D* in its center. This he rubbed like a talisman.

"The old man bought the place just for hunting. It's the only one he doesn't rent out." He stared at the pond, eyes narrowed. "The old man's quite a hunter. Just ducks, but they don't stand a chance." He raised an imaginary shotgun to his shoulder, aimed not at the sky but at the pond, and slowly squeezed back the trigger.

"Do you like to hunt?"

"Got enough of that in Korea."

"But you come here with your dad?"

"Oh, yeah." He cast her a humorless smile. "It's important to the old man."

He leaned back into the corner on his side of the car, resting his left arm on the top of the steering wheel, his right along the back of the seat. He studied Bess while she sat staring straight ahead, out the windshield, at the glowing shore where the lowering sun gilded all the cattails.

At length she turned toward him. "Do you come out here often?"

"You mean by myself?"

She nodded.

"Now and again. Never with a girl."

He continued to study her, and she turned away, observing, "It's beautiful and eerie. It must be hard going back to town."

"Sometimes I imagine that the town has disappeared. That I drive down the road and there's nothing there. Just fields."

"How would you feel if it disappeared?"

He thought for a moment, then shook his head. "I don't know." He grinned. "I don't know how I feel about a lot of things."

"That's why you went to Korea."

"Right. But that didn't last," he said, casting his eyes down at the leg that had gotten him discharged from the army. "And I'm all out of Koreas."

"Where does your dad keep his cattle? The purebreds? They're not here."

"South Dakota. Nebraska."

"Do you know a lot about cattle?"

"I guess someplace in my head I know a lot. The old man's tried to teach me." He frowned. "If I had to know it, I'd know it."

"How do you feel about working for your dad?" She loved asking him personal questions.

"Well, let's see. I like it better than shooting ducks." The corners of his mouth tweaked upward, but the smile went no further. "He needs me. I mean, I'm an only child. Who'd take over if something happened to him? My mom couldn't run the business."

Suddenly he climbed out of the car and strode away through the grass.

Bess watched, a little stunned, as he moved off tangentially toward a small promontory at the water's edge. Had she said something wrong?

CHAPTER 20

Harriet

"OF COURSE you're going to get married!" Kate snapped. "Bess had no right saying those things."

"It's not just that," Harriet sobbed, shaking her head. She hadn't shed this many tears since leaving Sioux City. And today was supposed to be a happy day.

"Well, that's what started it. You were happy as a schoolgirl when you left here with Rose. What Bess said made you start thinking and worrying."

"If I hadn't started thinking today, I would've started tomorrow or next week."

Again they were at the dining room table, though it wasn't yet time for supper. Kate had arrived home from Truska's to find Harriet making herself a whiskey drink in the kitchen, a thing unheard of except at the holidays. Beer now and then in hot weather. But whiskey on a weekday afternoon?

Harriet had run out of the kitchen when Kate and Frieda came in the back door, Frieda carrying Kate's box of groceries. Frieda had said, "I'll talk to you after supper."

Harriet was sitting at the dining room table, the drink before her, both hands clasped around it, as Kate walked in. Tears flooded an already blotched face, and Harriet grabbed a damp and crushed handkerchief lying beside the whiskey glass, dabbing at her eyes and cheeks. Her upper lip was swollen with crying and her shoulders trembled like a pile of dry leaves.

She couldn't stop crying. She'd thought that the whiskey would help, but she was having trouble drinking it. Her hands fluttered and wouldn't obey.

Her thoughts stumbled around, as unmanageable as her hands. If she went crazy, they'd send her to the state hospital in St. Peter. Well, maybe that was the place for her. She could finally stop worrying about everything—about Bess hating her for marrying DeVore; about DeVore's children hating her for trying to take their mama's place; about hanging on to a job that men had tried to take away from her (Why should *she*, they'd asked, an old maid with neither chick nor child, have a job that by rights belonged to a family man?). You couldn't hate someone who was in a state hospital.

"You've got to stop this," Kate was admonishing. "Nerves. That's all this is." She fetched a fresh handkerchief from a neat pile she kept in the sideboard next to the napkins. Tossing it across the table, she eased herself down onto a chair. "Wipe your face and stop this. I want to talk to you."

Harriet plucked up the handkerchief but crossed her arms on the table and buried her face in them, unable to stop sobbing. "Leave me alone." She'd never answered back to Kate that way, but she couldn't help herself. All the pain and confusion was making her crazy.

She didn't want to stay here at the table, going to pieces in front of Kate, but she didn't have the starch to get up and climb the stairs. She could imagine this unhappy moment expanding itself to fill the rest of her life.

"Maybe I *should* leave you alone," Kate said. "I don't know what good it does me to talk to you. You'll only believe what you want to." She frowned and picked up a big ceramic saltshaker, setting it down again, hard, as if it annoyed her. "But I *do* love you. And you had to earn that love. If you had enough good in you to earn my love, don't you think you've got enough to earn other people's?"

Kate's words traveled a great distance to reach Harriet, who was walking away from herself, abandoning the sappy woman sitting folded over the dining room table, the one who'd thrown herself a ludicrous business-college graduation party. She was putting distance between herself and all that misery, between herself and that woman's foolishness.

Kate's words barely reached her. Something about Bess loving her, about Bess not saying those terrible things unless she loved Harriet.

What did Kate know about *not* being loved? She'd never been homely as a mud fence. She'd married young, raised a pretty niece and a pretty grandniece, been loved by everyone. What did someone like that know about the absence of love or the awful importance of love? Didn't it require being loveless to know about love?

"You think everyone but you is strong and sure," Kate said, her voice sharp, "when really they're weak as babies and scared and kind of hungry all the time. But they strike a little path and put one foot in front of the other. It's a risk, but if you keep moving, you find things that need doing, things that you can put to rights. You get courage from moving." Kate rose and came around the table, laying a hand on Harriet's shoulder. "But you know that."

She shook the shoulder until Harriet lifted her head in protest. "Listen to me!" Kate insisted. "It doesn't matter if you do it for yourself or someone else. But keep moving.

"Hold on to people and let them hold on to you—this galloping Galahad of yours, what do you think he's doing but holding on to you?"

Kate moved away, grasping the back of a chair for support. With her free hand she covered her eyes as though they were shot through with pain. Harriet turned back from the corner where she'd retreated and stared at Kate's suffering.

Holding a handkerchief under her nose, she blubbered, "DeVore's boys don't want me. They laughed at me. And . . . and what do I know about being a mother?"

"The only thing you have to know is that those children need you." Kate lowered herself to the chair she'd been clutching. "They need someone to cook their meals and wash their sheets, someone who knows that they're scared half to death of forgetting their mother and losing their dad." Kate flung a folded napkin away from her as if to rid herself of this exhausting scene.

Wearily she said, "You could do that, Harriet, be that someone."

"But what about Bess?"

Kate sighed. "She probably won't speak to you. You're walking out on her. But after a year or two at college, she'll come around. I'd bet on it. And if she doesn't, that's *her* lookout. But don't use her as an excuse not to get married. She'd have it on her conscience for the rest of her life."

Harriet approached the poor heap that was herself and ran her hand over the creature's hair, smoothing it as she would a child's. Then she patted the woman's arm and stood trying to decide whether she loved her enough to put one foot in front of the other.

At length she rejoined herself and blew her nose, though it was not so much for love of herself as for Kate's sake. What had that been—Kate covering her eyes that way?

"And, my stars, Harriet," Kate said, her voice spent and reedy, "do you know how happy I'd be to have country people in the family again?" She struggled to her feet. "Now, wash your face."

In the kitchen Harriet turned on the cold water and splashed her face, soothing her burning eyelids and cheeks. When she was done, she dabbed her face with the hand towel. She would not cry anymore. DeVore was coming tonight to meet Kate. And whatever Harriet decided about him, she didn't want him to see that she'd been crying.

She really didn't know what she would decide. So many things were wrong with her marrying him. Why hadn't she seen that last night? She hadn't meant to toy with his affections.

She had been flattered to have him ask her. She'd thought it was what she wanted. But she'd been concentrating so hard on his asking that she hadn't thought about what it would mean. The worst, of course, was losing Bess. Kate could say what she wanted about Bess coming around, but Harriet remembered Mrs. Stubbs. Bess hadn't come around then.

And the expression on Bess's face today when she'd heard that Harriet was getting married. That wasn't something you'd soon forget.

Only minutes before, she had looked at Harriet as if she were someone *necessary;* they'd been so close, like mother and daughter, Bess feeding Harriet ice cream from her own spoon.

The first time that Bess had looked at her that way—as if she were necessary—was a couple of weeks after Celia and Archer's deaths. Kate had been down with a migraine (was that what she had today?) when Harriet came home from work, so Harriet had invited Bess out to supper.

They'd walked out to the highway and eaten at the all-night. Then, hiking home afterward, Bess had held on to Harriet's hand. And when they reached the Drew house and were sitting on the back steps, counting the early stars, seven-year-old Bess had turned to Harriet with much the same expression she'd worn this afternoon, a look of need and trust, and said, "Don't ever go to the Dakota Ballroom and drink too much, Harriet."

CHAPTER 21

Kate

WHEN SHE HEARD BESS at the front door, Kate pushed herself up from the kitchen stool.

The girl slipped silently into the hall and would have vanished upstairs, but Kate called out, "I'm ashamed of you."

Bess leaned heavily against the doorjamb. "What're you talking about?" she asked, her tone guarded, as if there might be more than one reason for Kate's shame.

"Harriet."

"I don't want to talk about Harriet. Harriet's dead." She started to turn away.

"Don't you dare walk away from me," Kate told her. "Are you going to kill off everybody who crosses you? I'll be the next to go."

"Oh for God's sake."

"I love Harriet."

"Well, good for you. I *don't*."

"You're a liar. You don't get off that easy. Come here and talk about this."

Bess made no move.

"What can it matter to you if Harriet gets married?

You're leaving for college in two weeks. But Harriet's got plenty of life ahead of her."

"Some life—married to a damned dumb farmer."

"Watch your mouth." If she were able to move, Kate would have shaken Bess until her teeth rattled. "I'm a farmer! You don't know anything about farmers! You're as ignorant as that Okie father of yours. And you don't know any more about love than he did."

"I know this much: if Celia were here, I'd have a lot more of it. *Celia* knew how to love people." Bess turned and bolted up the stairs.

Kate felt for the stool just behind her. Half an hour later she was still sitting at the kitchen counter and Celia was standing where Bess had stood.

"What to do?" Kate whispered, shifting on the stool to face Celia. "I forgot the things I meant to say. And what I did say was all wrong." She trembled with anger that was only now subsiding. "I wasn't much help to Harriet, either."

Upstairs Harriet was pushing hangers around in her closet, looking for the right dress. Right for what?

"What's going to happen when DeVore Weiss shows up?" Kate asked Celia. "Is she going to send him packing—her last chance for His and Hers bath towels and Mexican Surprise casserole and someone . . ."

Her breast heaved and she cast a glance ceilingward. Both of them, Harriet and Bess, were up there now, a few feet removed from each other, but as far apart as they would ever be.

"And where did Bess go after work?" Kate pressed Celia,

knowing she'd get no answer. No matter. Celia listened. The dead listened consumingly.

Bess had looked wary and covert when she came in, probably because she knew Kate would be angry with her. Kate recalled the girl in the dark-blue car, the one leaving Harvester when she and Frieda were returning. That girl had reminded Kate of Bess. She'd also reminded her of Celia, the way her body was turned toward the driver, inclined toward him, intent.

If the girl in the car was Bess, where was she going and who was taking her? Bess wouldn't tell Kate unless she wanted her to know. If she wanted her to know, it was because she had nothing to hide. What would she be hiding?

"My imagination's running away with me." It had been one of those deceptive glances. When you saw the car and the passenger again, you realized that there was little resemblance, only a trick of coloring and light. And what was wrong with a girl going for a ride in the country in the afternoon?

Kate lifted her arm, not an easy movement, and massaged the back of her head. Waiting for Bess to escape from Harvester, she'd got wound up as tight as the spring in a windowshade. She was growing dotty waiting.

Maybe the girl in the dark-blue car was a farm girl on her way home. Maybe she was one of the Geiger girls, whose family farmed the acreage neighboring the old Drew place.

If the girl were Bess and she rode past the Drew farm, would she realize that that particular land had been Kate and Martin's? Probably not. Bess had never taken an interest in the country side of Kate's life. Like many town girls, she looked down on farms. And farmers.

"You know how I miss the farm, Celia. Do you think Harriet understands what a blessing it would be to have country people in the family?"

Maybe Kate could teach Harriet a few things about the country. Naturally, things had changed in twenty-odd years, but some things didn't change, like slopping hogs and leading the cows in from pasture at milking time; gathering eggs from Plymouth Rocks and dressing Rhode Island Reds. Then, too, she'd subscribed to *Country Gentleman* for a good many years. She'd kept up and might still make herself useful.

At a quarter past seven she stood before the mirror in the front hall running a comb through her hair. Without dismay she thought, I look my age.

When she'd been a child newly moved to town, she'd looked at sixty-year-old town women like herself, gray-haired and not going anywhere except to Ladies' Aid meetings and to Lundeen's for a piece of cambric, and she'd thought that people who were sixty and settled heavily into their shoes had no concerns more serious than whether the squirrels would dig up the tulip bulbs. Life was simple and blessedly unworrisome for sixty-year-old women. By that age, your obsessions had subsided, and their memory was something soft to lay your head on.

But now she saw that sixty meant you knew more ways and more reasons to worry, and you knew how to swallow your worry each day, like a tiny dose of poison, while you sorted clothing for the missions and purchased your piece of cambric. At sixty your enduring obsessions burned as brightly as old stars.

Returning the comb to the drawer of the hall table, Kate made her way to the oak rocker in the living room, hooking her cane over the arm. From there she watched for DeVore Weiss, her eye eager and worried.

At seven-thirty a car stopped in front of the house, and a tall, loose-jointed fellow, wearing tan twill trousers and a freshly pressed plaid cotton sport shirt, emerged, one long leg at a time.

He slammed the car door, started up the walk in a headfirst lope, remembered something, and returned to the car. Retrieving a box from the front seat, he headed again for the house. So thoroughly scrubbed and pressed was DeVore Weiss, he looked as if he were on his way to church.

The doorbell shrilled, and Kate grabbed her cane, struggling to her feet. "I'm coming. I'm coming."

"How do, Mrs. Drew." He grinned broadly. "I'm a natural poet, don't ya think? 'How do, Mrs. Drew.'" He stuck out his hand, and Kate shook it.

"I'm Kate," she told him, leading him into the living room, liking him already. Why on earth had Harriet thought that he had only one expression? "Have a seat there, on the sofa."

He held out the box he carried, a Whitman's Sampler. "This is for you."

"A bribe, is it?"

"Well, of course. What kind of fool do you take me for?" he laughed, and Kate laughed with him.

If she were younger, Kate thought, she might marry this long-legged German herself. "I'll call Harriet. You open this box so we can all have some." She went to the hall and called up the stairs, "Harriet, you have a guest." Then she returned to the living room, helped herself to a caramel, and resumed her seat in the rocker.

"You farm east of town," she said.

"Yes, ma'am. I farm a full section three miles east."

"That's a lot of land."

"I've got a couple of high school boys and a good hired man. It's plenty of work, though."

"You like it?" Kate pressed.

"I wouldn't want to do anything else."

She relaxed. "I lived on a farm when I was small, and again when I was married. There isn't a better life."

"I hope you'll be spending time out at our place once Harriet and I make it legal."

"I'd like that." Where was Harriet? Why wasn't she down here entertaining this lovely fellow? "Would you like a glass of iced tea or a beer, Mr. Weiss?"

"I'm just plain DeVore to you. And I'd like a glass of beer. It's been hotter than a gangster's pistol all day."

When Kate returned with the beer, Harriet had come down and was standing in the doorway. She wore a cotton dirndl skirt covered with pink and lavender flowers, and a soft, gathered peasant blouse. The garments made her look rounder and very womanly.

"DeVore and I have been having a nice chat," Kate told her. "Now he's going to have a beer. Why don't you come sit on the sofa?"

DeVore was standing and he gestured toward the empty space beside him on the sofa. Harriet crossed the room shyly and, straightening the back of her full skirt, sat down, but leaving a distance of perhaps twelve inches between herself and DeVore.

Now what, Kate wondered. Should she get out of the way or try to cement them together in some conversational way? "DeVore's been telling me he farms a section. That's a big farm."

"Six hundred and forty acres," Harriet piped, like the bright little girl who has researched on her own.

"Yes. A man surely needs loyal, hard workers with a spread like that," Kate observed. "DeVore, maybe Harriet would like one of the Whitman's chocolates you brought. I had a caramel and it was delicious. DeVore was saying maybe I could visit the two of you when you're settled. Nothing would make me happier. You know how I am about the country. If you invited me out once in a while, I'd think I'd died and gone to heaven." Had she laid it on too thick? she wondered.

"Well, of course, we want you to spend as much time with us as possible," Harriet affirmed indignantly, as if the point had been questioned. "You'll be one of the family, won't she, DeVore?"

Holding the Whitman's Sampler box on her lap, Harriet bent over the chart on the inside of the lid, while running a finger lightly along the rows of chocolates.

"Anything wrong?" DeVore inquired.

"I'm looking for a maple-flavored piece."

DeVore slid over next to Harriet and bent his head over the chart. "Looks to me to be the second from the end in this row," he said, handing her a piece of candy.

"No, that wasn't it," Harriet told him, chewing and swallowing the candy. "That was mint. I didn't think it was the right shape for maple."

"Well, I think you'd better just eat through that row until you find it," DeVore suggested.

Kate decided that it was time to go. Besides, her hands weren't quite steady; she needed to put her head down. "I think I'll go upstairs now," she told them. "I've had a busy day. I hope to see you often, DeVore."

CHAPTER 22

Bess

BESS SOAKED in the lily-of-the-valley-scented bath for forty minutes while the pads of her fingers grew raisiny. As the water cooled, she added warm. Harriet had already had her bath when Bess arrived home, so she needn't worry about relinquishing the tub, not that she would any longer worry about such things. Harriet could look out for herself.

The rooms were not soundproof, and Bess could hear Harriet dressing to go out, could hear hangers making little metallic *snick-snick* sounds, scraping back and forth across the closet pole. Harriet was on edge.

Aunt Kate had said that she was ashamed of Bess. Why? Because Bess had tried to save Harriet from a terrible mistake, whereas Kate was letting her go without a qualm, easy come, easy go?

Harriet belonged *here*. Coming home from college to find her gone would be like coming home to find her dead. No, worse than that, because she would have gone willingly.

If Harriet turned down DeVore Weiss, would she be so *very* miserable? She couldn't feel about him the way Bess felt about Doyle Hanlon. Who knew what Harriet felt—desperation? Embarrassment at being unmarried? Whatever it was, it was turning her into some German galoot's hausfrau.

Still, Bess knew with certainty that Harriet would marry DeVore Weiss and move to a farm east of town and look after three or four subhuman Weiss children. She wouldn't any longer be Bess's family. She would be Mrs. DeVore Weiss.

Bess's fists clenched beneath the scented water, its lily-of-the-valley bubbles long since collapsed.

Like Celia and Archer, Harriet was lost to Bess. Bess squeezed her eyelids tight. She wouldn't cry over Harriet. Though she still mourned Celia and Archer when they sneaked up and stood hovering at the boundaries of sleep, she sure as hell wasn't going to mourn Harriet.

Aunt Kate was calling up the stairs to Harriet, telling her that she had a guest. Harriet bounded down the hall, past the bathroom door, high heels clacking on the wooden floor. Down the stairs she hurtled, sounding like a many-cornered object falling, step to step, all the way to the bottom.

Bess yanked the rubber plug by its chain, and the bathwater began slurking away. Rising, she reached for a towel and stood for a moment watching the water line sink lower and lower, leaving no ring because the bubble bath carried it away. In just that way would Harriet disappear from Bess's life, leaving no residue.

Bess dried off and pulled on an old robe. She tried to glide soundlessly down the hall lest Aunt Kate be reminded that she was home and ask her to come down when she was dressed. She wouldn't come down for DeVore Weiss.

Anyway, they were probably having a lovely time, all of them talking about *her*. Or about DeVore's farm. Aunt Kate would like that. She was obsessed about the country, about "the old place." Bess didn't even know where the old Drew place was. Kate must have pointed it out to her once, but she couldn't remember.

Bess flicked from its hanger a green cotton sheath dress that Harriet had sewn for her from a Butterick pattern. One of her favorites, it set off her black hair and dark eyes. Never again would Bess stand on the dining room table, laughing and complaining, while Harriet took half an hour to mark a hem with the talcum powder marker. "For God's sake, Harriet, this style will be out of fashion before you get the hem marked."

Bess lay down on the bed and held the corner of the sheet to her eyes. She was still lying on the bed when she heard her great-aunt, slower and more hesitating than usual, climb the stairs.

At the top, Kate waited, as though catching her breath or gathering strength. At last she started down the hallway, but creeping, it seemed to Bess, her cane going only a little ahead of her with each step. When she passed Bess's room, she didn't pause or call or knock. Bess could sense the high feeling on the other side of the door as Kate passed. Her aunt must be very angry. Maybe Harriet had told DeVore no, and it was Bess's fault.

In the thickening twilight, Bess stared at the sloping

ceiling, thinking how much she had lost in twenty-four hours: Harriet, maybe Kate, maybe even Donna when she figured out what was going on between Bess and Doyle Hanlon. Well, it was their loss.

In the quiet gray depths of the first floor, the phone was ringing. She waited for Harriet to answer, but the ringing continued. Bess got up and ran down the stairs. Was it Doyle Hanlon calling to change their plans?

When she reached the phone, it had stopped ringing. She didn't dare call the operator to ask who had phoned. If it were Doyle Hanlon, she could not risk arousing the suspicions of the women at the telephone company. Sue Ann Meyers's mother might be on the switchboard tonight.

Bess went to her room and put on stockings and flat-heeled shoes. Turning on the light over the makeshift vanity, she applied mascara and lipstick; then, pulling her hair into a ponytail, she twisted it into a French knot and pinned it in place.

Digging in a shoe box under the vanity, she found a pair of earrings made to look like green jade flowers with gold leaves. Screwing them on, she cast an oblique glance at the person in the mirror, someone alien to her, someone with old eyes, Archer's eyes.

She flicked off the light and left the room, pulling the door to and glancing down the hall at her great-aunt's closed door. She wouldn't knock. Aunt Kate might be asleep. At the foot of the stairs, Bess hesitated, turning to look back up into the shadows of the landing.

On the dining room table she saw a big Whitman's Sampler box. Extracting a nut cluster, she stood chewing thoughtfully, shifting her weight from one foot to the other, tapping with her fingertips on the back of a chair. At length she crossed to Kate's desk and sat down, switching on the fluorescent desk lamp and drawing a notepad to her.

Aunt Kate—In case you get up in the night and come downstairs—Gone to meet Donna. I love you and I'm sorry you're ashamed of me. Too much of Archer in me, I guess. Bess.

Gazing around the dining room as if it might be a long time before she returned, she picked up her purse from the table. At the front door, she flipped the porch light on, closing the screen door silently behind her.

The sky was still a fading delphinium color, but the streetlights were lit and the evening star was bright. Bess walked south on Second Street. She didn't want to encounter Cousin Frieda. Aunt Kate had said nothing about seeing Bess in a dark-blue Mercury that afternoon, but perhaps Cousin Frieda would bring it up. Panicky circumspection was a part of Bess now. You never knew when you might slip up.

She stepped along almost on tiptoe, not calling attention to herself. A milky full moon, pale and innocent, hung low in the eastern sky, evoking Celia's face. All gentle curves and softness, Celia had kissed her good-bye on the steps of Aunt Kate's house, then driven away, framed in the open window of the car, smiling at Bess as she disappeared out of sight. Everywhere she turned these past two days, Bess was met by Celia. Bearing right, onto First Avenue, Bess turned her back on the Celia moon.

As she reached Truska's, she stumbled without apparent cause, thrust out a hand to steady herself against the brick wall, then sank down on one of the steps leading to the side door. Bent over double, she held her fingers in the corners of her eyes and bit her lower lip.

"Bess! I've been looking all over for you. I called your house and no one was home." Donna was hurrying across Main Street, waiting for a car to pass, then running on toward her.

Bess straightened.

"I wanted to talk to you at the cafe," Donna explained, advancing toward her. "But with Shirley hanging around, there wasn't any chance. Let's sit here a minute." She was breathing heavily. "Where're you going? You're all dressed up."

"I was heading for the Lucky. I got a stitch in my side," she lied, "so I sat down. Sometimes I think I have an appendix problem."

"Why didn't you call me after work?"

"I got tied up. I'm sorry."

"Doyle Hanlon?" Donna asked without warning.

"What do you mean?"

"I don't know, but something's going on with you and him, that's all. The way you acted last night. Then his dropping in at the cafe and leaving when he didn't see you. I've got a funny feeling." Donna lay a hand on Bess's. "Am I wrong?" she asked.

Bess shook her head. She looked at Donna, then away. "Please don't tell anyone."

"Why would I? When did this all happen?"

"Last night . . . today. It's hard to believe it happened so fast. You probably think I'm a tramp, but it's still *me*, Donna. I'm so scared."

Donna put her arms around Bess. "Would you like me to go with you to the Lucky?"

"Yes. We'll give you a ride home."

"This doesn't change you and me," Donna told her as they walked. "We're still friends."

Bess was too grateful to answer.

"I'm not going to college," Bess told Donna when they had settled into a booth and ordered beer.

Donna said nothing, but she was shocked, Bess could see. She was more shocked by this than by Bess's confession about Doyle Hanlon.

"I can't leave."

"What about your aunt Kate?" Donna asked. "She's all excited about you going to college. She told me how proud she was that you were a good student."

"If I stay, I can look after her. Harriet's marrying DeVore Weiss."

"Wonders never cease."

"Aunt Kate's going to be alone, and I don't want to leave. It seems like something that was meant, doesn't it?"

"But she's going to think it's *her* fault you're not going."

"I'll make up some story so she'll know it's nothing to do with her."

Hammy brought their beers and carried away the

dollar bill Bess had laid out. "What'll you do if you stay, work at the Loon?" Donna asked.

"I don't know."

"There aren't any decent jobs around unless you've got a college education."

"I haven't had time to figure everything out."

"I think you should go to college. You can see him on weekends. If it's really love, it'll last."

"For God's sake, Donna, you sound like some damned Joan Fontaine movie."

She regretted hurting Donna's feelings, but she couldn't stand to hear glib inanities about love from someone who didn't know the first thing about it.

At that moment Doyle Hanlon pushed open the screen door and cast a glance about as though casually surveying the room for anyone he might know. Only a dozen other customers were scattered around, and they were all from the Ula National Guard unit on their way home from training in St. Bridget.

When Doyle Hanlon's eyes found Bess and Donna, he assumed an expression of pleased surprise. Stopping at the bar to pick up a beer, he made his way along to the girls' booth.

"Well, ladies, we meet again. May I join you?"

During the next hour Doyle Hanlon danced twice with Bess and twice with Donna. To an observer he appeared to be whiling away an innocent Thursday evening.

Seeing him touch Donna and laugh with her drove Bess wild. She wanted to punch them both. How much worse it would be if the woman were his wife. And it was inevitable in such a small place that Bess would see them together.

The first time that Bess danced with Doyle, she told him that Donna had guessed at something between them. "But she won't tell anyone," she assured him.

He did not appear panicked. He only said, "We'll have to be discreet."

Bess's anxious spirit revived. He wasn't going to tell her tonight that he couldn't see her again.

At ten Bess and Donna left by themselves. By agreement, Doyle remained behind long enough to finish his beer, then climbed the iron stairs to the street and got into his car. The girls waited on the step by the side door of Truska's Grocery Store.

"Isn't he perfect?" Bess whispered.

"He's very good looking."

"Oh, I know, but it isn't his looks. I mean, not mainly his looks. But whatever it is, it makes my chest ache, as though somebody'd hit me in the breastbone. And my hands shake. And I feel kind of dizzy all the time, as if I might stagger when I get up to walk."

"Sounds like a disease." Donna giggled.

Bess shuddered. "Yes."

"Have you . . ."

Bess shook her head.

"Will you?"

"I don't know."

Doyle Hanlon drove up and they rode off, Bess in the middle, Donna on the outside. For those few minutes, driving to Donna's house, a feeling of cozy conspiracy existed between them. Bess felt tender gratitude toward Donna and she leaned across to hug her friend as Donna opened the door in front of her house.

"Be careful," Donna called softly as she waved.

Doyle headed the car north out of town on the road to Ula, but instead of turning around in Ula, he kept on going, into the country, to a roadhouse where they knew no one and where they could dance. He grabbed an opened fifth of bourbon from the glove compartment of the car and carried it into Ed's, as the place was called.

They ordered charged-water setups and two bags of potato chips. Doyle left money on the table for the setups and walked across the room to the jukebox. Bess's glance followed, drugged by his tapering back. She wanted to take off his clothes and kiss the scar that must adorn his thigh from his motorcycle accident.

They drank and danced close, Bess's arms around his neck, his around her waist. She was happy.

Occasionally, Doyle's breath grew harsh against her ear and she thought that he wanted to make love to her and that he would suggest leaving. But then he would order another setup. Finally he said, "I'm afraid of hurting you."

"I don't see how that can be avoided," she told him. "It would be worse if I couldn't see you."

Did being in love with Doyle Hanlon mean that she was a girl of bad character? She'd always assumed that such girls chose and enjoyed their sins. She had not chosen to love Doyle. And it would never be in her power to choose not to.

There was no place for this to go, no end for it but grief.

When she saw the end coming, she would leave him. She couldn't live if he left her first. Maybe she couldn't live anyway. She pitied herself and Doyle Hanlon. And Celia and Archer and Harriet and DeVore. She pitied everyone who loved. How did they find the grit to gamble so heavily, and what made it worth the losses? Bess did not believe that anyone ever won. And yet, they played.

"Last call," the bartender announced at a quarter to one.

Doyle ordered and at a quarter past one they left. In the car he reached for her. His kisses weren't slobbery but light and tender as shortcake. Bess was impatient to go where they invited, however much it hurt. The thought of its hurting pleased her. Years from now maybe he would recall her pain and find a strange comfort in it, a proof that she had cared.

"I want you," he whispered against her hair and lay her hand between his thighs where he was hard. "But say no, if you're frightened."

Beneath the layers of his clothing Bess felt a vein throbbing as insistently as her own pulse. She knew little about real lovemaking. What did he want her to do? She ran her hand lightly over him.

He sighed, laying his forehead against her shoulder. After a moment, he raised his head slowly, as if the movement cost him much concentration. Looking at her directly, he said, "You have to be sure. It'll be very wrong if you're not sure. I'm not that selfish. I hope I'm not."

"If all the happy minutes of my life were rolled together, they wouldn't amount to this," she said.

He started the car. Silently they drove back through the hushed streets of Ula and on south toward Harvester, turning into the same rutted farm lane as in the afternoon. The Mercury bucked and slewed like a rowboat on a stormy sea as it veered left past the vacant farmhouse. The moon followed them, casting a gauzy mantle over the spectral landscape. Was Archer up in the moon with Celia, his face peering out from the dark side?

CHAPTER 23

Kate

KATE HEARD BESS LEAVE. She was too upset with the girl to call out, to ask where she was going or when she would be home. Now she regretted it. She hated anger between herself and Bess and Harriet. When they quarreled, she did not want one of them to leave, especially to go in a car, without someone calling out, "Be careful," and someone else answering, "I won't be late."

She lay fully clothed on the bed and dozed. About ten she woke breathless with panic, then weepy with self-pity because she was helpless.

"Calm down," she whispered. But panic, she knew, did not yield to reason. Sometimes it yielded to light or movement.

Inching toward the edge of the bed, she willed her legs over the side. In the bathroom she washed her face and slipped into a soft muslin gown, a creeping uneasiness replacing the panic.

Bess had been furtive today, watchful, and guilty in her manner. Was she guilty of something beyond her horrid behavior toward Harriet? Something to do with the dark-blue car?

Hooking her cane around the cross brace of a straight-back chair, Kate dragged it the few feet across the linoleum floor to the bathroom sink and sat down, resting her arm along the cool surface of the porcelain.

Should she call Donna Olson's house? Was Bess even with Donna? No, she wouldn't call, not at this hour. If Bess was there, she was safe; if she wasn't, Kate had no idea where she might be. The Dakota Ballroom had no dances on Thursday. At length Kate braced herself on the sink and pushed up from the chair.

The air was cooler downstairs. The windows were all open, and the doors as well. A breeze might come up later. Maybe she would sleep on the daybed on the front porch.

With the dim light of the street lamp to guide her, she settled into a wicker rocker on the porch. The elms, faithful nocturnal companions, twitched in discontented sleeplessness, rough leaves whispering, relaying messages borne to them on the heavy night air. Kate sat rigid, alert, listening.

At midnight DeVore Weiss's car pulled up in front of the house. Kate looked away and debated whether she should try to creep into the living room. She didn't want Harriet thinking that she was spying. But the pain in the back of her head had returned, an elephant's foot crushing her skull. She closed her eyes and waited.

Fifteen minutes later Harriet and DeVore got out of the car and, conversing softly, made their way arm in arm up the walk to the door. She had not turned him down.

They said good night, Harriet calling after him, "Sleep tight." Opening the screen door, she stepped in, humming "A Bushel and a Peck."

"Harriet." Kate tried not to startle her, but that was impossible.

"My, but you gave me a start!" Harriet told her, holding a hand to her heart and advancing onto the porch. "Is anything wrong?"

"Bess isn't home, and I couldn't sleep, so I came downstairs. I wasn't spying. I closed my eyes when you pulled up."

"For crying out loud, you don't need to explain. Should I make cocoa?"

"No, it's too warm, thank you. Go to bed. You have work in the morning."

"I'm not sleepy. I feel like I could stay up all night. I sent DeVore home because he has to get up before the birds."

"Did you have a good time?"

"Yes. We went to *The Quiet Man* and then to the Lucky Club for a beer. Hammy Kretzmarsky said that Bess and Donna had been in and left. Bess is probably at Donna's. Those two can jaw for hours."

"Yes," Kate agreed, but she was not reassured. "Did you set the date?"

"Valentine's Day."

"Perfect."

"Did Bess say anything after I left?" Harriet wondered.

"I lay down. We didn't talk."

"You shouldn't fall asleep early in the evening. That's why you can't sleep now."

"Perhaps."

"DeVore really took to you."

"You tell him if I was twenty years younger, I'd set my cap for him."

The daybed springs mewled as Harriet sat down and pulled off her high heels. "I've been thinking about Bess."

"Don't worry about her. When the time comes to be happy, you can't put it off. You're doing the right thing. And you won't be rid of me, you know."

"Oh, I know. Where would I get the courage to be a farm wife if I didn't have you to teach me?"

"Get to bed now. You'll be exhausted in the morning. And the girls down at work won't give you a minute's peace."

Rising, Harriet gathered up her pumps and purse from the floor, crossed to the rocker, and kissed Kate's cheek.

Kate had not expected it, and it shook her.

"Don't wait up for Bess," Harriet told her. "Heaven only knows when we'll see her."

One o'clock. Knives twisted in Kate's hips. Thank goodness the rocker was easier to get out of than most chairs. You could propel yourself forward with its motion, as she did now, rising to her feet, bent over, holding the arms until she could grab the cane and get it under her.

Straightening, she dragged along into the house. Once she was moving, things got easier. Passing her desk, where a small fluorescent lamp burned, Kate noticed a sheet of paper on the blotter.

Aunt Kate—In case you get up in the night and come downstairs—Gone to meet Donna. I love you and I'm sorry you're ashamed of me. Too much of Archer in me, I guess. Bess.

Kate stared long at the note, then stuffed it into the pocket of her robe. "Poor little girl," she whispered, crossing to the wall switch and flicking on the overhead light. "Poor little girl."

Opening the top drawer of the sideboard, she withdrew a deck of cards and carried them to the dining room table. Seated, she riffled through the deck, extracting the face cards and aces, returning the others to the box. With the face cards and aces she began laying out a pattern of forecasting that Elsie had taught her all those years ago, some cards facedown, others up. Pausing again and again, she held the unused cards against her chin as she studied and considered, then continued.

When the sixteenth and final card was revealed, she made a little "unhh" sound in her throat and sat for some time poring over the people and events lying before her on the table. At last she gathered up the cards, returning them to the box and the box to the drawer.

In the kitchen she set the kettle on to boil and withdrew three small jars from the Hoosier cupboard, each labeled *Kate's*. Unscrewing the lids with difficulty, she measured a teaspoon of dried herbs from each jar into a china teapot. When the kettle whistled, she filled the pot with boiling water. While the infusion steeped, she crossed to the open door, staring out toward the back drive and the alley, where the shapes of lilac bushes were a denser black than the rest. Somewhere, Bess was in a car, a dark-blue car, with a man Kate did not know.

Too much of Archer in me . . .

Kate poured a cup of tea, flicked off the kitchen light,

and headed toward the darkened living room, setting the cup down on the lamp table. Removing the little blue volume of mythology from the bookcase, she turned on the reading lamp and lowered herself to the sofa, to one side so that she could use the arm to push herself up again. Wetting the tip of her twisted index finger on her tongue, she paged through the book until she found the tale of which she never tired.

"And Demeter braved the Stygian gloom . . ."

Later, setting the book aside, she turned off the lamp and sat in darkness. "Celia," she breathed. When she heard the word, she sighed again, "Celia," as though it were a charm or invocation. For two days Celia's spirit had beat itself against her like a branch beating itself against a window in a storm.

Kate sipped the tea until it was mostly gone, then set the cup aside, and closed her eyes.

The moon, like a huge china plate, is hanging high in the western sky, lighting her way. She wears a coarse muslin nightgown bleached white as the moon by many washings. On her feet, everyday shoes, thick and sturdy and worn, pick their way through pasture grass, stepping around rocks and cow pies. Following the path trampled by the cows, she holds her hem high to prevent its being dirtied by manure or soaked by the dew lying thick on the grass.

The moon paints the pasture with hoarfrost though the August night is hot and breathless. She has left the stifling bedroom to come looking for air. There is none to be had, but there is space. Space is almost like breeze.

Not only heat and breathlessness were stifling her in

the bedroom, but also fear. She can count on the fingers of one hand the number of times in life when she has been afraid. But the thought of the man in the gray fedora jellifies her bones.

He isn't a cattleman, though Martin says he owns cattle; he surely isn't a farmer despite the farms he's bought up. He's a man who owns things, that's all he is, a man who owns things.

Martin has talked with him. She could not prevent it. But he has promised not to decide anything until the harvest is in. Nevertheless Kate is half-mad with fear. She paces the pasture in the dark of night, the grove in the heat of day. Back and forth, back and forth, in ever-shrinking paths, as if walls are being thrown up against her on every side.

She angles around the west side of the pond, then marches along the northern perimeter until she reaches the place where the creek spills out at the eastern end. The cattle come down to the water here, especially in summer, a thin line of willow and cottonwood offering shade. The ground is muck where the cows have slogged in the damp earth.

On the opposite side of the creek, between herself and the house, the grove of cottonwoods rises up, leathery leaves capturing light from the brilliant moon. Mosquitoes are thick and buzzing, but they do not bother Kate.

She stops short. Abruptly, as if summoned, she turns and runs, returning in the direction from which she has come, the moon before her. She rounds the western end of the pond, heads back along the cow trail and into the yard. Out at the road, lights veer into the long lane.

Loping and lunging, slowly they come, two huge and

blinding predator eyes. So late. Who would come in the middle of the night? Trouble. Only trouble comes in the middle of the night. The man in the fedora is coming to steal from them when they are most vulnerable and weary.

She sprints headlong, not minding her feet now, but hurtling forward down the lane toward the light. Flinging out her arms to block the way, she cries, "Go back! Back to town! Don't come here." She pitches herself at the car's radiator. The hood ornament strikes her breast and the car hurls her backward.

CHAPTER 24

Bess

IT SOUNDED AS IF THEY'D HIT A BIG ROCK. Doyle braked the Mercury suddenly, and Bess threw out her hands to brace herself against the dashboard. Seizing a flashlight from the glove compartment, he leapt from the car without a word and unlatched the hood.

Now what? Bess wondered dreamily, resting her head against the seat.

Doyle shone the light into the vital organs of the car. The Celia moon had been dragged halfway down the sky by its own great weight, so that the car lay in the night shadows of the box elder grove, headlights burning. Luna moths fluttered up, dashing themselves against the lights.

"Shit," Doyle muttered.

"What is it? What's wrong?"

"I'm not sure. I think I've thrown a rod."

"Can we fix it?" She could help. She'd learned a little about cars from Mr. Wheeler in driver's education.

"No way. Not if it's a rod."

"What'll we do?"

He slid back into the front seat and slammed his fist against the steering wheel. "Shit." Closing his eyes, he swallowed the bile of his anger.

"Could we get a farmer to help us?"

"At this hour? The two of us? Anyway, what could he do except give us a ride into town?" By noon the news would be all over the county. Doyle Hanlon and Bess Canby. Doyle's wife would hear. And his parents. With a deep intake of night air, his anger escaped in a long rough breath, while the taste of resignation lay on his tongue, savorless as month-old bread.

"I can't stay out all night," she told him. "Aunt Kate'll call Constable Wall."

"You'll have to walk back to town." He switched off the lights and ignition. Night crept up close.

"Alone?"

"There's nothing to be afraid of."

"I'm not afraid. It's just . . . never mind. How far is it, five miles?"

He nodded. "I'm sorry," he said. Right forearm extended through the lower loop of the steering wheel, he batted the keys hanging from the ignition, giving them a last impatient swat. "I'm as green and half-grown as when I enlisted," he said with disgust, withdrawing the arm and laying his hand on Bess's thigh. "I've made a mess of this."

"What will *you* do?" she asked.

"Sleep in the old house. We've got cots out here for hunting season. I'll walk to the Geigers' farm in the morning and call the garage."

"What'll your wife think when you don't come home?"

"Won't be the first time." He squeezed Bess's thigh. "Lotta times I can't sleep, I run away. Out here. Not as dramatic as Korea, but handy." A bruised expression came over him, and he held tight to Bess's leg, unaware that his fingers were digging into her flesh. "Just stay a minute."

She did not care about the small pain to her thigh. "I have to go," she said. She had to get home before daylight.

Running a hand down her cheek and along her jaw, he traced her lips with his fingertips.

She snatched them between her teeth, biting down until she knew that she was hurting him.

"I'll walk you to the road," he told her.

They stumbled along the lane, where foxtail and thistle cleaved to them as they passed. Each with an arm around the other, they held fast, she to his waist, he to her shoulder, squeezing too hard, claiming and punishing each other.

At the road they clung for a moment, then thrust each other away without a word. Words were containers for small and tidy feelings.

Bess ran.

Gathering a black scum of mascara and road dust, tears channeled down her face unnoticed and uninterrupted.

She could not run for long. After hurtling headlong for a mile, turning her ankles again and again on the coarse gravel, her heels were bleeding where the shoes raised blisters and then punctured them. She stopped on the grassy verge between the road and the ditch and stepped out of the flats. Unhooking her garter belt, she skinned that off, along with the nylons, stuffing them into the shoes. Then, snatching up her clutch bag in one hand and the shoes in the other, she ran.

How long before the sky would pale?

Because the road would cut her feet to pieces, she was running on the grass now. But even the grass was full of gravel thrown up by cars. Again and again she cried out and hobbled.

Winded, she slowed, gulping air and kneading her side where a sharp stitch pinched. In the deep grass of the ditch bottom and along the fencing, things moved. When she slowed, she could hear them. Thinking about them was less distressing than thinking about Doyle Hanlon, so she considered the hidden, scurrying animals. Rabbits, gophers, raccoons. Maybe a fox. Snakes probably.

Far ahead, separating themselves from the dim string of lights that were Harvester, two brighter lights blossomed. A car. God, she couldn't let the driver see her.

Throwing herself down into the ditch, she waited, praying that the deep grass and the green sheath dress would conceal her. She damned the time it took the car to approach, precious minutes when she should be running.

With the car well past, Bess emerged, dashing ahead, trying to gain lost time. She was approaching the Geigers' farm, where yard lights burned and a dog barked, a large dog by the sound of it.

As a driveway opened up between dark flanking trees, the dog came plunging down the lane, barking and growling. A huge black creature, he bounded into the road at Bess's heels, snapping and snarling.

She could run no faster. Her chest ached and the vein in her temple wanted to explode. Again and again the dog lunged at her heels, each time a little closer, working up the will to sink his teeth into her fleshy calf. She felt his slobber on her skin.

Across the road, on the right and ahead of Bess, lay a small grove not attached to a farmhouse. From these trees rose a howling that broke off abruptly into barking. As Bess and the black dog drew near, another dog appeared, behind the far fence, crawling beneath it to emerge at the top of a little incline. He hesitated, then flew down into the ditch and up to the road's edge.

The new dog ran along the opposite verge, foraying now and then onto the road, snarling. Not all dogs in the country belonged to someone. Dogs who'd been abandoned and turned feral roamed across farms, killing small animals and scavenging.

The lights of town were brighter, closer, maybe two miles distant, but Bess could not go on running. Soon she would have to stop. The cramp in her side was screwing itself deeper into her belly so that she ran hunched to that side.

As the second dog charged out farther onto the road, the Geiger dog responded, gnarling and snapping at him, veering out from behind Bess to drive the other dog back, yet never abandoning his pursuit of her.

Sweat poured from Bess's scalp, down her back, and down her brow into her eyes. At first she thought that the two lights expanding on the horizon were no more than salt stinging her eyes, but they flared up into headlights. Once more she threw herself into the ditch.

Now the dogs would be on her. When they saw that

they'd run her to earth, they would leap on her. Could two dogs, one of them wild, kill a person?

Celia, help me. Fly out of the moon.

She hooded her head with her arms and lay gasping, throat on fire. The car was coming fast. Someone drunk, speeding home.

And then it was passing, tossing up dust and hurling gravel, roaring ahead, driving the darkness back. The dogs pursued its exhaust, leaping to snatch its heels, falling back and leaping again, finally falling off, still barking and contending far down the road, where their voices waned.

Bess did not move. She listened. Close at hand crickets screaked, admonishing her to go home where she belonged; mourning doves, disturbed in their rest, murmured deep in their throats, unarticulated and motherly advice.

When she had regained her breath, Bess dragged herself up and set out limping, first at a walk and then a trot and then again a walk. At the outskirts of Harvester, town dogs set up a tune, but these were behind fences or tied up. Bess trotted raggedly along Pine Street, turning at last down Third Avenue. A slatey horizon silhouetted the trees on the east side of town. How many people, behind curtains, observed her passing, purse and shoes in hand?

At Second Street she crossed diagonally to the left toward Aunt Kate's house. Except for the light cast by the streetlamp, the house lay in predawn darkness. Maybe Kate was still asleep.

Letting herself in, Bess tiptoed along those floorboards that she knew didn't squeak. Straight ahead through the foyer she crept, and then into the dining room to lay her bag on the table so that Kate, when she came down, would know that Bess was home.

Gliding down the upstairs hallway, she heard Harriet's soft snoring. Outside her own door, Bess glanced toward her aunt's, where thin, lace-filtered light from the streetlamp reached across the room and through the open door. But Kate's bed was lost in the darkness.

With the soiled green sheath flung down in the closet, bloodied flats beneath it, Bess pulled on a cotton gown and shivered despite the heat. Sliding into bed, she drew the sheet over her and lay cold and still as stone.

Slogging home had required all her strength and attention. But now she must pick over the past several hours, gingerly, like someone tending a wound.

She saw that the car trouble had closed off some gap in a wall through which Doyle Hanlon had hoped to squeeze, however briefly. Possibility had drained out of him as he sat cursing his luck. Not merely the possibility of their making love—maybe that was the least of it—but some other possibility that she could not define.

Her head throbbed.

Climbing out of bed and padding to the bathroom, she swallowed three aspirin and let the cool water run in a trickle while she wet a flannel cloth. Lifting it to her face, she saw in the mirror the ravages of the night's tears. With care she bathed the swollen eyes, the puffy cheeks and tumid mouth.

Doyle Hanlon isn't done with wishing, but he is done with daring.

I would have dared.

Harriet shook her head and put her arms around Bess, her throat so tightly closed off that she couldn't speak.

"I don't believe you," Bess said, shrugging the woman off.

"I found her when I went downstairs. I've called Gus and Archie Voss." The constable and the mortician. "And Dr. White and Frieda." Had she forgotten anyone?

"I'm still dreaming," Bess cried, throwing back the sheet and pushing Harriet aside. "Aunt Kate!" she shrieked, running to Kate's room. Faced with an empty bed, she wheeled, racing into the hall and down the stairs. "Aunt Kate!"

Harriet followed, dabbing her eyes dry with the tissue and cinching her robe.

Kate was sitting on the living room sofa, head thrown back, arms flung out to either side, one resting on the sofa arm, the other on a seat cushion, as if—as if what? As if she had been thrown there with great force, Harriet thought.

Bess knelt and reached out tentative hands to lay them on Kate's knees. "Aunt Kate." She stroked the cool, lifeless hand lying on the sofa.

Harriet stood in the doorway. "I closed her eyes."

"Oh God," Bess moaned and lay her head on Kate's knees.

Steps sounded on the front porch. Frieda and Arnold. Stripped of all her starch and looking as if her rough, sturdy knees might give way, Frieda came first, still in hair curlers and carrying a cake pan.

"I had this coffee cake . . ." she said, holding out the pan, as if offering it to a lifeless Kate.

When Harriet had taken the cake from her, Frieda

stood, her thick, reddened fingers held prayerfully at her waist, as if she were at the Communion railing. "I told her I'd call her after supper. But we went to *The Quiet Man*."

Harriet said, "I'll put this in the kitchen and start some coffee." She hesitated. Was Frieda all right? Should she fetch the ammonia?

"Sit down, Frieda," Arnold told his wife, guiding her to a chair.

Frieda obeyed, though her gaze remained fastened on Kate. She shook her head as if Kate's pose puzzled her. Aloud but to herself she said, "She doesn't look frightened, does she?"

Bess still knelt at Kate's feet, clinging to her aunt's knees.

Carrying the coffee cake to the kitchen, Harriet filled the electric percolator, adding a few grains of salt to the coffee as Kate always did to bring out the flavor. When she'd plugged in the perc, she sat down on Kate's stool.

She was no Kate, but she would be the best Harriet she could be. She had to consider that wild and willful little girl in the living room.

However much she came to love DeVore's children, they would never mean to her what Bess did. Wasn't it strange, maybe even wrong, how a person loved the unlovable one fiercest of all?

Someone knocked softly at the screen door, and Arnold went. "Gus."

Within minutes the doctor and the mortician followed the constable into the house, bringing with them the stamp of certitude. Indeed, Kate Drew was dead. Harriet drew

Bess away from the body so that Archie Voss and Gus Wall could lift Kate onto a gurney, cover her with a sheet, and wheel her out to the waiting hearse.

Still in her nightgown, Bess followed, out the front door, down the steps and the sidewalk to the street. Harriet pulled her back before she could climb into the hearse.

"She shouldn't be alone," Bess cried.

Holding the girl, Harriet stroked her long, disordered hair. *What she means is* she *shouldn't be alone*. Harriet was pleased with herself for recognizing this. It was the sort of thing that Kate would have seen.

When the hearse had disappeared, Harriet led Bess inside, telling her, "Why don't you have a bath while I make breakfast for Frieda and Arnold? Frieda looks like the frayed end of a rope."

Later, when she had bathed and dressed, Harriet sat down at Kate's desk to draw up a list. If you didn't know what to do, if you were half-crazy, the best thing to do was draw up a list. Taking up a pen, she wrote, "People to Call." DeVore. The new Methodist minister, Reverend Hinks. Well, new a year ago. Dry as dust, but the best that they had.

Then she must call the nursery about floral sprays. And what about the Ladies' Aid Circle? They'd need to know. They'd be helping with the reception after the service. Come to think of it, she had to notify a lot of people. Mr. Hardesty at the *Standard Ledger*. Oh, no, he was on vacation. That new young reporter, then. And so on and so on. Good thing she had a head for detail.

Harriet knew better than to trust this composure. She

was running on disbelief. But that was all right, a sight better than collapsing and crawling into bed, which was what she wanted to do.

Her several lists completed, she climbed the stairs. From Kate's closet she withdrew a couple of dresses, laying them across the unmade bed.

"Bess," she called, "could you come here?"

Bess appeared, looking sightless. Though she wasn't crying, her face was puffy and flushed as if stung all over by bees.

"Which of these dresses do you think I should take to Voss's?"

"The dark red was her favorite."

Returning the blue dress to the closet, Harriet said, "You might want to come to Voss's with me."

"What're you going to do?"

"Well, the most important thing is to pick out a casket." Harriet swallowed hard.

For Bess the content of Harriet's words lagged far behind the sound. "Yes. All right," she said after several moments.

Before they left Voss's but after they'd concluded their business, Archie Voss brought out the gown and seersucker robe Kate had been wearing, handing them to Harriet.

"Would you like these?" Harriet asked Bess.

Bess took them, observing that her note to Kate was sticking partway out of the robe pocket. *Aunt Kate—In case you get up in the night . . .* someday she would be glad that Kate had read her note. But now, nothing mattered except that Kate was dead. In the night without farewell or trumpets.

Bess was disconnected, untethered. That Kate had been her tether all these years only now occurred to her. She must hang on to things if she was not to float away entirely. In her room she picked up books from the floor and from the bed and held them for ballast. Returning them to the shelf, she held on to the bookcase as if to a mooring.

When she had returned all of the books, she gathered up the many items of clothing lying scattered, clasping them to her as though their mass and history lent them weight. Laying them in the laundry basket, she stood beside the closet door, clutching the basket in her arms.

At length she set the laundry down beside the door and pulled the sheets and pillow slips from the bed, dumping them in with the soiled clothes.

Climbing onto the bed, she clung to it for half an hour.

In Kate's room later, she saw the unmade bed, hardly rumpled because Kate was unable to fling herself about. *Had been* unable to fling herself about. Lifting Kate's pillow, Bess held it against her face, breathing in the scent of Pond's cold cream and Lady Esther dusting powder.

"Would you like to sleep in here now?" Harriet asked from the doorway.

Eventually the question reached Bess. Without turning, she said, "Yes."

"Should I change the linens? I'm doing some wash."

"No. Thank you."

Still holding the pillow, Bess sat down on Kate's little bedroom rocker, the one in which Kate had rocked Celia when Celia was small, singing lullabies to her and reciting nursery rhymes. Bess knew this because Celia had told her and because Kate had done the same for Bess when she was small.

"The Queen of Hearts
She made some tarts,
All on a summer's day.
The Knave of Hearts
He stole the tarts,
And took them clean away.

"The King of Hearts
Called for the tarts,
And beat the Knave full sore;
The Knave of Hearts
Brought back the tarts,
And vowed he'd steal no more."

Throughout the day neighbors brought food. The funeral was set for Monday, a long way off, but no one wanted it on Sunday. Harriet hoped the casseroles and cakes would keep until the wake Sunday night. She'd carried several dishes over to Marie Wall's to store in her refrigerator and several to Frieda's.

Between phone calls and visits, Harriet tried to keep an eye on Bess. At noon she called her down for a little lunch. Bess came willingly enough, but she only drank iced tea and ate a bit of watermelon, not enough to keep her strength up.

Later, Harriet rang Mrs. Olson, who had already heard about Kate from Marie Wall. Maybe Donna could talk to

Bess, Harriet thought. Maybe she could find out if Bess was, well, all right. But Donna was babysitting. She had a job for the summer, baby-sitting part time while the mother filled in at the Friendship Arms Nursing Home. Harriet had forgotten.

With the wash hung out on the line, Harriet donned an apron, tied a scarf around her head, then fetched the Hoover, dust mop, and rags from the closet in the kitchen. In the living room she gathered up the pile of *Country Gentlemans*, wondering where to put them. "Well, of course," she said aloud and carried them up to her room, stacking them on top of the *Better Homes and Gardens*.

Cleaning house felt sacrilegious to Harriet, but, like washing clothes, it answered the need to be doing something.

After supper Donna showed up. In the living room on the sofa, in the very spot where Kate had died, Bess heard Harriet tell her, "She's in there. Go ahead in."

"I'm real sorry about Kate," Donna said from the door.

Receiving no answer, she crossed to the sofa, sitting down at the opposite end. No one had turned on a lamp, and the east-facing room, with a porch in front of it, was thick with dusk.

"Was it a heart attack?"

At length Bess cleared her throat. "I guess."

"Did you know she had a bad heart?"

Bess shook her head slowly.

"When exactly did she die?"

"Probably between one and three this morning, Dr. White said."

They sat in silence, then Donna asked, "Were you home?"

Again, Bess shook her head.

Donna leaned toward Bess to study her face. Bess turned toward her but she was floating, not connecting. Donna edged closer, taking Bess's hand.

That was better, Bess thought.

For half an hour they sat like this, not talking. Harriet came in to flick on a lamp but, seeing the girls together on the sofa, thought better of it and left. Somewhere in the back of the house, voices murmured, a syllable or two drifting now and then through the dining room and into the living room, arriving too diminished to be recognizable. Both the kitchen and yesterday lay miles distant.

In a low voice Donna asked, "Did you find Kate when you came home?"

"No." Bess sighed. "I didn't look in here. This is where . . ."

"What time . . . ?"

"Nearly four-thirty."

Donna stirred but did not let go of Bess's hand.

Bess's voice was nearly inaudible. "Nothing happened," she said, answering the unasked question. "Nothing is going to happen."

When Donna left, the two girls walked to the door hand in hand. Afterward Bess was again without anchor.

In Kate's room she sat on the bed, her back against the metal headboard, hugging the pillow to her. She wanted to think about Kate, to caress, like rosary beads, memories of her aunt, but her mind wouldn't grasp hold of memory.

Much later, Harriet stood at the bedroom door, silhouetted by the hall light. "May I come in, little girl?"

"Yes."

"Gracious, it's warm in here," she said, switching on the electric fan on the chifforobe.

Harriet perched on the edge of the rocker. "DeVore was here. He said to tell you how sorry he is. And Arnold and Frieda. I don't think Frieda's stopped crying all day. I'd have thought she would be stronger than any of us. I told Reverend Hinks that you were resting." Harriet eased back into the rocker and folded her hands in her lap.

"I let Frieda bring the wash in," she went on. "She folded the towels and washcloths, and sprinkled the ironing. She's coming over tomorrow to scrub the kitchen floor and iron. She'll make herself sick if she doesn't stop. But she has to be doing something. For Kate, I guess."

Harriet fell silent. She got up and crossed to the bed, laying her hand on Bess's hair, reeling the girl in from that place in the ether where she drifted. When she spoke again, Harriet was more hesitant.

"Arnold and DeVore and I talked while Frieda was taking care of the wash. The men said there were things I should tell you, and of course they were right. First of all, this house is yours, and you don't have to decide this minute what you want to do with it. When you go to college, we'll look after it. I'll be living here till next Valentine's anyway, and after that Arnold and Frieda will keep an eye on things."

College? Bess thought. What college was that?

"If you decide sometime down the road that you want

to sell the house, you will always have a place with me and DeVore or Frieda and Arnold. We all want you to know that."

She bent and kissed Bess's cheek. "Try to sleep."

And indeed Bess did fall asleep, waking in the deepest cave of night to shamble along in the dark to the bathroom, half-asleep and still wearing the skirt and blouse she had worn to Voss's Funeral Home. She turned on the bathroom light, putting a hand up to shield her eyes from the glare. When she had used the toilet, she shucked off her clothes and pulled on the nightgown draped over the rim of the tub, where she had left it.

Rinsing her face and brushing her teeth, she padded back down the dark hall, not bothering with a light, noting as she passed Harriet's open door the rhythmic drone of Harriet's oscillating fan.

From Kate's room came a low voice, nearly lost in the hum of electric fans. Harriet must have gotten up and come in while Bess was in the bathroom.

At the door, Bess paused. Only now were her eyes growing accustomed to the darkness. "Harriet?"

The voice in the far corner grew more distinct:

"I saw a ship a-sailing,
upon the silver sea;
And, oh! it was all laden
with pretty things for thee!"

Bess grabbed for the doorjamb and clung to it.

"There were comfits in the cabin,
and apples in the hold;
The sails were all of silk, dear Bess,
the masts were made of gold."

"Celia?" Bess breathed.

She crept forward. Behind the rocker, outside the watery shaft of streetlight, stood Celia in her mauve cotton dress, pale face gazing down on the baby in Kate's arms.

". . . all laden with pretty things for thee!"

Wearing her white muslin gown, Kate laughed and cooed:

"The Knave of Hearts
Brought back the tarts,
And vowed he'd steal no more."

"Aunt Kate?" Neither figure glanced up.

Bess's fingers pleaded to touch them, but they might melt. Never taking her eyes from them, she climbed into bed and lay listening.

". . . And vowed he'd steal no more."

Blinking hard again and again, Bess tried not to sideslip across the boundary of wakefulness. But at twenty minutes to two, by the luminous hands of the Big Ben, she was coaxed across the frontier into seamless sleep.

CHAPTER 26

Kate

LIKE THE MOON, Kate was leached of sharp-edged existence in daylight. Yet soundlessly she tramped the box elder grove, embracing limb and bole.

From the grove she saw the gray Dodge raise dust a mile down the road. As it turned into the lane, she drifted toward that spot in front of the house where Frieda always parked.

Waiting for the dust to settle before opening the car door, Frieda observed, "When folks came Sunday for the wake, wasn't there a lot of 'em standing around outside, though?—men like to do that when it's warm and then they can smoke and talk—and the yard looked real pretty. That was nice, that you mowed the grass and weeded Kate's little garden. She would like that." Climbing out of the car and clamping on her straw hat, she said, "Harriet's a good girl, but she's not much in the yard."

Surveying the tangled box elder grove, the equally tangled cottonwood grove down by the pond, and the great patch of weeds that was the farmyard, Frieda shoved her lower lip firm against the upper one and set her substantial jaw, her eye stern and defiant.

Bewildered, Bess opened the passenger door and emerged, tentative and apprehensive.

"Your Aunt Kate's farm," Frieda said.

"*This* . . . is where she and Uncle Martin farmed?" Leaning against the car door, Bess surveyed the farmyard as though for the first time.

"Yah. This is it." Frieda rounded the front of the car. "And up here by where Kate had her garden, the old folks are buried, Martin's mama and papa. I'll show you," she called, plowing through the sea of weeds like a staunch frigate.

Bess started after her, glad she had worn jeans. The weeds were tall and thick and clung with prehensile tenacity.

"Here's where Kate had her big garden," Frieda explained, marching off a great swath of yard. "And over here's the graves." She waved Bess to follow.

Nothing marked the two side-by-side plots but the rocks outlining each. And the rocks would be impossible to find if you hadn't memorized the location.

After several moments' consideration, Bess said, "They're my great-great-aunt and -uncle by marriage."

"Well, I don't know, but maybe you're right. Shirttail relation of some sort." Snatching the handkerchief from the bosom of her dress, Frieda mopped her forehead and waved the cloth in the air to drive back the gnats. "Relations are important. Kinda like a map of where a person is and where they been, don'tcha think?

"People should pay respect," she went on. "This is a disgrace." She waved her straw hat at the overgrown grave sites. "Kate used to tend 'em years ago when she was able, before the arthritis. After that I told her I'd do 'em, but old Hanlon who owns the place put up a gate with a lock on it at the top of the lane and a NO TRESPASSING sign, and Kate said she didn't want me out here climbing the fence."

Bess had knelt and was pulling the weeds on the graves and tossing them aside.

"We still drove past every chance," Frieda told her, "but it hurt Kate not to walk here, to check how things were."

"Why didn't somebody ask Hanlon's permission?"

Frieda, too, was on her hands and knees now, pulling weeds. Flinging a great handful down on Bess's pile, she stared off toward the lane. "Arnold asked. Hanlon said *he* would be the one liable if someone was to get hurt out here. Just an excuse. He's one of those people has to have his way."

Bess snatched vicious handfuls of weeds, ripping them from their beds and hurling them down.

"Year or two ago, we was driving past," Frieda said, "and the lock was gone."

Something pinched Bess's brow. She held a clutch of weeds in front of her face for a moment as if to smell the sunlight and green life escaping from them.

"You getting a headache?"

"No." Furtively Bess wiped her eyes on the back of her forearm, then resumed weeding.

Ten minutes later Frieda sat back, laughing. "Are we two crazy women?" she asked, mopping her brow again and glancing at the considerable pile of weeds. "Look what we done. The old folks can see out now."

"When I come home from St. Cloud next summer, I'll take care of the weeds," Bess told her. "And I could plant flowers."

"Maybe something perennial that don't need watering every day. Yarrow and daylilies, maybe."

When they had cleared the graves of weeds and neatened the rock borders, Bess wandered up to the house. Cupping her eyes, she peered in several windows at rooms mostly empty. Only the kitchen showed signs of use. Arranged around the old wood-burning cookstove were two cots, army blankets folded neatly at their feet, a table, and two chairs. An open cupboard door hanging loose on its hinges revealed boxes of shotgun shells, glasses, and a bottle of Johnnie Walker.

Bess lingered for several minutes at the kitchen window before Frieda asked, "You want to see the pond?"

Kate followed Bess and Frieda, her presence no more intrusive than the zephyr fluttering the cottonwood leaves, revealing their dull undersides and loosening a handful of harbinger leaves, though this was only the twenty-seventh of August.

After Indian summer she would leave. Or not. She would leave when she'd finally gotten her fill of the place, when she had swallowed it whole like oysters and grown sated. Would such a time come? Such a fullness?

At the little rise beside the pond, Frieda brushed away mosquitoes and cast a caretaker's sweeping glance over the scene. A tumult of Canadian geese rose from the pond, crying last-minute exhortations and instructions to one another. Aloft, they slipped and shifted into a *V* and headed south, sinuous necks straight and straining as they towed autumn in their wake.

Trailing her cousin, Bess knelt suddenly, drawn by something lying in the weeds. A silvery disc with a raised letter *D* in the center.

Glancing at Frieda's back, she wiped the charm on her jeans, then slipped it inside her bra to lie against her breast.

When Kate had watched them drive away, watched them down the road past the Geigers' farm, she strayed across the yard to the sagging porch, trussed recently and without craft—no commitment, only expediency, use, and a belief in paper: mortgages, liens, deeds.

Spreading her arms wide and swallowing deep draughts of a landscape worn and patinated, she considered the persuasions of heaven. She might have to forgo them.

WITH GRATITUDE to Lee Boudreaux, my editor at Random House, for her wisdom, skill, and unfailing good humor. Thanks as well to the knowledgeable, dynamic Douglas Stewart, agent and friend at Curtis Brown, Ltd.

And, finally, a continuing thank—you to my husband, Dan, and our three children—Maggie, Ben, and Kate—all writers themselves. Their patience, support, and example have availed and inspired me.

Sandra Kjarstad Bloom

FAITH SULLIVAN is the author of eight novels, including *Good Night, Mr. Wodehouse* and *The Cape Ann*. A "demon gardener, flea marketer, and feeder of birds," she is also an indefatigable champion of literary culture and her fellow writers, and has visited with hundreds of book clubs. Born and raised in southern Minnesota, Sullivan lives in Minneapolis with her husband, Dan.

Interior design by Connie Kuhnz
Typeset in Warnock Pro
by Bookmobile Design and Digital Publisher Services

Warnock Pro was designed by Robert Slimbach for Adobe Systems. A classic font style with a contemporary feel, Warnock Pro has become a staple of book and magazine design.